TH   GE

DR   ND

ROBERT LOUIS STEVENSON

WORKBOOK BY ANNE ROONEY

PEARSON

YORK PRESS

YORK PRESS
322 Old Brompton Road, London SW5 9JH

PEARSON EDUCATION LIMITED
Edinburgh Gate, Harlow,
Essex CM20 2JE, United Kingdom
Associated companies, branches and representatives throughout the world

First published 2016

10 9 8 7 6 5 4 3 2

ISBN 978–1–2921–3808–4

Illustrations by Jeff Anderson; and Rob Foote (page 48 only)

Phototypeset by Carnegie Book Production
Printed in Slovakia

Photo credits: © iStock/Dadzoola for page 15 / © iStock/ElementalImaging for page 17 / konstanstinks/Shutterstock for page 23 / © iStock/ElementalImaging for page 25 / © SuperStock/Corbis for page 28 / MrFisher/Shutterstock for page 29 / © iStock/gianliguori for page 61 / © BARNETT; H WALTER/AS400DB/Corbis for page 62

CONTENTS

PART ONE:
GETTING STARTED

PART TWO:
PLOT AND ACTION

PART THREE:
CHARACTERS

PART FOUR:
THEMES, CONTEXTS AND SETTINGS

PART FIVE:
FORM, STRUCTURE AND LANGUAGE

PART SIX:
PROGRESS BOOSTER

PART ONE: GETTING STARTED

Preparing for assessment

All exam boards are different, but whichever course you are following, your work will be examined through these three Assessment Objectives:

Assessment Objectives	Wording	Worth thinking about ...
AO1	Read, understand and respond to texts. Students should be able to: • maintain a critical style and develop an informed personal response • use textual references, including quotations, to support and illustrate interpretations.	• How well do I know what happens, what people say, do, etc? • What do I think about the key ideas in the novella? • How can I support my viewpoint in a really convincing way? • What are the best quotations to use and when should I use them?
AO2	Analyse the language, form and structure used by a writer to create meanings and effects, using relevant subject terminology where appropriate.	• What specific things does the writer 'do'? What choices has Stevenson made? (Why this particular word, phrase or paragraph here? Why does this event happen at this point?) • What effects do these choices create? Suspense? Mystery? Drama?
AO3	Show understanding of the relationships between texts and the contexts in which they were written.	• What can I learn about society from the book? (What does it tell me about attitudes to science in Stevenson's day, for example?) • What was society like in Stevenson's time? Can I see it reflected in the text?

If you are studying OCR then you will also have a small number of marks allocated to AO4:

AO4	Use a range of vocabulary and sentence structures for clarity, purpose and effect, with accurate spelling and punctuation.	• How accurately and clearly do I write? • Are there small errors of grammar, spelling and punctuation I can get rid of?

Look out for the Assessment Objective labels throughout your York Notes Workbook – these will help to focus your study and revision!

The text used in this Workbook is the Penguin English Library edition, 2012.

How to use your York Notes Workbook

There are lots of ways your Workbook can support your study and revision of *The Strange Case of Dr Jekyll and Mr Hyde*. There is no 'right' way – choose the one that suits your learning style best.

1) Alongside the York Notes Study Guide and the text	2) As a 'stand-alone' revision programme	3) As a form of mock-exam
Do you have the York Notes Study Guide for *Dr Jekyll and Mr Hyde*? The contents of your Workbook are designed to match the sections in the Study Guide, so with the novella to hand you could: • read the relevant section(s) of the Study Guide and any part of the novella referred to; • complete the tasks in the same section in your Workbook.	Think you know *Dr Jekyll and Mr Hyde* well? Why not work through the Workbook systematically, either as you finish chapters, or as you study or revise certain aspects in class or at home. You could make a revision diary and allocate particular sections of the Workbook to a day or week.	Prefer to do all your revision in one go? You could put aside a day or two and work through the Workbook, page by page. Once you have finished, check all your answers in one go! This will be quite a challenge, but it may be the approach you prefer.

HOW WILL THE WORKBOOK HELP YOU TEST AND CHECK YOUR KNOWLEDGE AND SKILLS?

Parts Two to **Five** offer a range of tasks and activities:

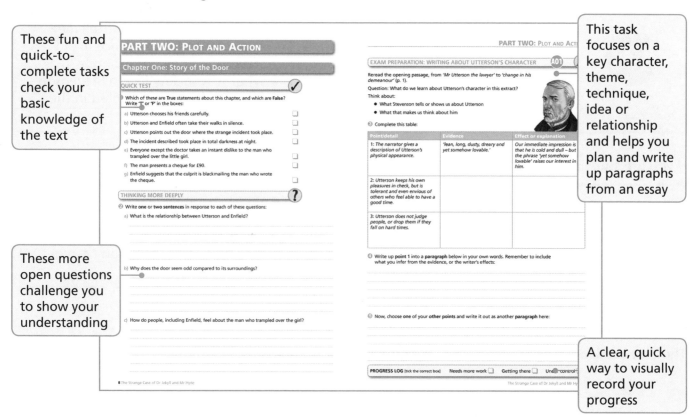

These fun and quick-to-complete tasks check your basic knowledge of the text

These more open questions challenge you to show your understanding

This task focuses on a key character, theme, technique, idea or relationship and helps you plan and write up paragraphs from an essay

A clear, quick way to visually record your progress

Each Part ends with a **Practice task** to extend your revision:

An exam-style task for you to practise a full essay

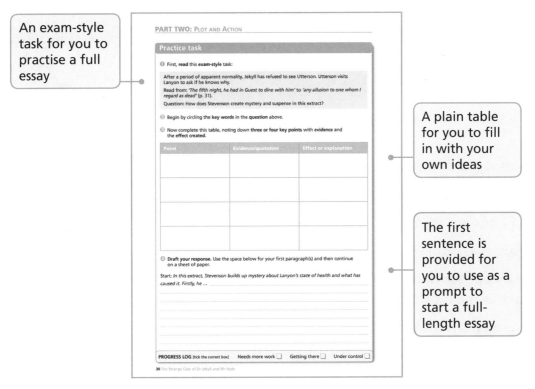

A plain table for you to fill in with your own ideas

The first sentence is provided for you to use as a prompt to start a full-length essay

Part Six: Progress Booster helps you test your own key writing skills:

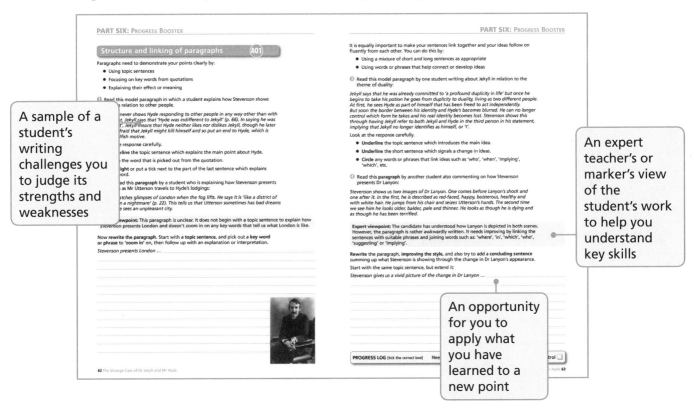

A sample of a student's writing challenges you to judge its strengths and weaknesses

An expert teacher's or marker's view of the student's work to help you understand key skills

An opportunity for you to apply what you have learned to a new point

Don't forget – these are just some examples of the Workbook contents.
Inside there is much, much more to help you revise. For example:

- lots of samples of students' own work at different levels

- help with writing skills

- advice and tasks on writing about context

- a full answer key so you can check your answers

- a full-length practice exam task with guidance on what to focus on.

PART TWO: Plot and Action

Chapter One: Story of the Door

QUICK TEST ✔

❶ Which of these are **True** statements about this chapter, and which are **False**?
Write **'T'** or **'F'** in the boxes:

a) Utterson chooses his friends carefully. ☐

b) Utterson and Enfield often take their walks in silence. ☐

c) Utterson points out the door where the strange incident took place. ☐

d) The incident described took place in total darkness at night. ☐

e) Everyone except the doctor takes an instant dislike to the man who trampled over the little girl. ☐

f) The man presents a cheque for £90. ☐

g) Enfield suggests that the culprit is blackmailing the man who wrote the cheque. ☐

THINKING MORE DEEPLY ?

❷ Write **one** or **two sentences** in response to each of these questions:

a) What is the relationship between Utterson and Enfield?

....
....
....
....

b) Why does the door seem odd compared to its surroundings?

....
....
....
....

c) How do people, including Enfield, feel about the man who trampled over the girl?

....
....
....
....

EXAM PREPARATION: WRITING ABOUT UTTERSON'S CHARACTER **A01**

Reread the opening passage, from *'Mr Utterson the lawyer'* to *'change in his demeanour'* (p. 1).

Question: What do we learn about Utterson's character in this extract?

Think about:

● What Stevenson tells or shows us about Utterson

● What that makes us think about him

③ Complete this table:

Point/detail	Evidence	Effect or explanation
1: *The narrator gives a description of Utterson's physical appearance.*	'lean, long, dusty, dreary and yet somehow lovable.'	*Our immediate impression is that he is cold and dull – but the phrase 'yet somehow lovable' raises our interest in him.*
2: *Utterson keeps his own pleasures in check, but is tolerant and even envious of others who feel able to have a good time.*		
3: *Utterson does not judge people, or drop them if they fall on hard times.*		

④ Write up **point 1** into a **paragraph** below in your own words. Remember to include what you infer from the evidence, or the writer's effects:

....

....

....

....

⑤ Now, choose **one** of your **other points** and write it out as another **paragraph** here:

....

....

....

....

PROGRESS LOG [tick the correct box]   Needs more work ☐   Getting there ☐   Under control ☐

Chapter Two: Search for Mr Hyde

QUICK TEST ✔

❶ Choose the **correct answer** to finish the statement and **tick the box**:

a) Dr Jekyll's will is very strange because:

it leaves all his money to Mr Hyde ☐   it provides for Jekyll's disappearance

as well as his death ☐   he has given it to Utterson to look after ☐

b) Utterson visits Dr Lanyon to ask:

why he has fallen out with Dr Jekyll ☐   whether he still sees Dr Jekyll ☐

if he knows who Hyde is ☐

c) Utterson can't sleep at night because:

he is worried that Jekyll is being blackmailed ☐

he is annoyed that he learned nothing useful from Lanyon ☐

he is irritated by the contents of Jekyll's will ☐

d) Hyde becomes angry with Utterson because:

Utterson stopped him when he was busy ☐   Utterson recognised him ☐

he thinks Utterson has lied to him ☐

THINKING MORE DEEPLY ?

❷ Write **one** or **two sentences** in response to each of these questions:

a) Why has Lanyon fallen out with Jekyll?

....

....

....

....

b) How does Utterson feel when Poole tells him that Jekyll is not at home?

....

....

....

....

c) What does Utterson think is happening between Jekyll and Hyde?

....

....

....

....

EXAM PREPARATION: WRITING ABOUT HYDE

Reread the passage from *'The lawyer stood awhile'* (p. 13) to *'that of your new friend'* (p. 14).

Question: How does Stevenson present Utterson's views on Hyde?

Think about:

- Utterson's impression of Hyde
- The language used to convey his impression

❸ Complete this table:

Point/detail	Evidence	Effect or explanation
1: *Hyde is unattractive, but his physical appearance does not account for the unease that Utterson feels.*	*'not all of these together could explain the … disgust, loathing and fear with which Mr Utterson regarded him.'*	*This creates a sense of mystery and suspense for us as readers.*
2: *Utterson feels that Hyde is somehow deformed, but cannot say how.*		
3: *When we hear Utterson's own voice on the topic of Hyde, it is uncharacteristically emotional.*		

❹ Write up **point 1** into a **paragraph** below in your own words. Remember to include what you infer from the evidence, or the writer's effects:

....

....

....

....

....

❺ Now, choose **one** of your other points and write it out as another **paragraph** here:

....

....

....

....

....

....

PROGRESS LOG [tick the correct box]   Needs more work ☐   Getting there ☐   Under control ☐

Chapter Three: Dr Jekyll was Quite at Ease

QUICK TEST ✓

❶ Complete this **gap-fill paragraph** about the chapter, with the **correct or suitable information**:

Utterson stays behind after dinner because he wants to talk to Jekyll about his

.... Jekyll begins talking about Lanyon. Although this looks like a

distraction, it is important as it gives the other side of the ....

between Jekyll and Lanyon. Jekyll considers Lanyon to be .... and

pedantic. Jekyll is .... when Utterson begins to talk about Hyde.

He claims he can be .... of Hyde whenever he wants to, but begs

Utterson to .... Hyde when Jekyll has disappeared. Utterson is

.... but agrees.

THINKING MORE DEEPLY **?**

❷ Write **one** or **two sentences** in response to each of these questions:

a) Why do Utterson's friends like him to stay behind at the end of an evening's entertainment?

....

....

....

....

b) How does Jekyll respond when Utterson says that he has learned a bit about Hyde?

....

....

....

....

c) Why does Utterson say 'I have no doubt you are perfectly right' when that is not what he really feels?

....

....

....

....

EXAM PREPARATION: WRITING ABOUT JEKYLL'S SPEECH A02

Reread the passage from *'It can make no change'* to *'let it sleep'* (p. 18).

Question: How does Stevenson use Jekyll's response to Utterson to develop different aspects of the story?

Think about:

● What Jekyll says

● The way he expresses it

③ Complete this table:

Point/detail	Evidence	Effect or explanation
1: *Jekyll is keen not to offend Utterson while refusing his help.*	*'this is very good of you, this is downright good of you'*	*Jekyll needs Utterson to be on his side as he is relying on him to carry out the terms of his will.*
2: *Jekyll is evasive, and Stevenson uses this to increase the mystery and suspense.*		
3: *Jekyll responds with 'a certain incoherency of manner' which Stevenson conveys in the way that Jekyll speaks.*		

④ Write up **point 1** into a **paragraph** below in your own words. Remember to include what you infer from the evidence, or the writer's effects.

....

....

....

....

⑤ Now, choose one of your **other points** and write it out as another **paragraph** here:

....

....

....

....

....

....

PROGRESS LOG [tick the correct box]   Needs more work ☐   Getting there ☐   Under control ☐

Chapter Four: The Carew Murder Case

QUICK TEST ✔

❶ Who is each character talking about? **Write a name** from the list below next to **each quotation**:

Utterson   **the maid**   **Mr Hyde**   **Sir Danvers Carew**

Dr Jekyll   **the landlady**   **Inspector Newcomen**

a) Inspector Newcomen: 'He don't seem a very popular character' (p. 23)   ....

b) Narrator: 'an aged and beautiful gentleman with white hair' (p. 20)   ....

c) Utterson: 'I had better tell you who this person is' (p. 23)   ....

d) Narrator: 'It seems she was romantically given' (p. 20)   ....

e) Narrator: 'She had an evil face, smoothed by hypocrisy; but her manners were excellent.' (p. 23)   ....

f) Utterson: 'who was much of a connoisseur' (p. 23)   ....

g) Narrator: 'he was conscious of some touch of that terror of the law' (p. 22)   ....

THINKING MORE DEEPLY ?

❷ Write **one** or **two sentences** in response to each of these questions:

a) How does the maid come to witness the attack on Sir Danvers Carew?

....

....

....

....

b) Why do the police come to Utterson after finding the body of Sir Danvers Carew?

....

....

....

....

c) What is the inside of Hyde's apartment like?

....

....

....

....

Reread the passage from *'It was by this time about nine'* to *'assail the most honest'* (p. 22).

Question: How does Stevenson make use of the famous thick London fog?

Think about:

- How the scene is described

- What it contributes to the atmosphere

③ Complete this table:

Point/detail	Evidence	Effect or explanation
1: *Stevenson describes how the fog swirls and changes, and is not a constant thick blanket.*	*'Mr Utterson beheld a marvellous number of degrees and hues of twilight.'*	*The movement and patchiness of the fog make it possible for Utterson to catch fleeting glimpses of the scene it hides.*
2: *The fog makes daytime as dark as night.*		
3: *Stevenson describes the fog in a way that makes things unclear and inconsistent.*		

④ Write up **point 1** into a **paragraph** below in your own words. Remember to include what you infer from the evidence, or the writer's effects.

....

....

....

....

⑤ Now, choose one of your **other points** and write it out as another **paragraph** here:

....

....

....

....

....

....

PROGRESS LOG [tick the correct box]   Needs more work ☐   Getting there ☐   Under control ☐

Chapter Five: Incident of the Letter

QUICK TEST ✓

① Which of these are **True** statements about this chapter, and which are **False**? Write **'T'** or **'F'** in the boxes:

a) Guest is an expert in working out a person's character from their handwriting. ☐

b) Utterson is worried that Jekyll might be protecting Hyde in his house. ☐

c) Guest agrees that the person who wrote the note must be 'mad'. ☐

d) Utterson has frequently been in Jekyll's laboratory. ☐

e) Jekyll has learned of the murder from Poole. ☐

f) There is fog even inside Jekyll's house. ☐

g) Utterson meets Jekyll in the sitting room of Jekyll's house. ☐

THINKING MORE DEEPLY ?

② Write **one** or **two sentences** in response to each of these questions:

a) Why does Utterson suspect that Jekyll has forged the note from Hyde?

....

....

....

....

....

b) How does Utterson respond to seeing Jekyll's cabinet?

....

....

....

....

....

....

c) What is Jekyll's response to the murder of Carew?

....

....

....

....

....

....

....

EXAM PREPARATION: WRITING ABOUT SETTING A02

Reread the passage from *'It was late in the afternoon'* to *'in a changed voice'* (p. 25).

Question: How does Stevenson present Dr Jekyll's laboratory?

Think about:

- Contrasting features of the laboratory
- How it is described

❸ Complete this table:

Point/detail	Evidence	Effect or explanation
1: *The laboratory was once a dissecting theatre, but is presented by Stevenson as livelier then than now.*	*'once crowded with eager students and now lying gaunt and silent'*	*The contrast between the room's gloominess now and the dissecting theatre is surprising and sets the scene for dismal events.*
2: *The room is not cosy; it is full of equipment, is dimly lit and has barred windows.*		
3: *The fire and lamps are lit, yet still the room is dark and cold.*		

❹ Write up **point 1** into a **paragraph** below in your own words. Remember to include what you infer from the evidence, or the writer's effects:

....

....

....

....

....

❺ Now, choose one of your **other points** and write it out as another **paragraph** here:

....

....

....

....

....

PROGRESS LOG [tick the correct box]   Needs more work ☐   Getting there ☐   Under control ☐

Chapter Six: Remarkable Incident of Dr Lanyon

QUICK TEST ✔

❶ Choose the **correct answer** to finish the statement and **tick the box**:

a) After the murder of Carew, Jekyll becomes:

gloomy and solitary ☐   sociable and charitable ☐   lively and fun-loving ☐

b) Utterson thinks that Lanyon has changed because he is:

afraid he is going to die ☐   sad to have fallen out with Jekyll ☐
old and weary ☐

c) Jekyll writes to Utterson because he:

is tired of Utterson's attempts to visit ☐   wants to explain everything ☐
is responding to Utterson's letter ☐

d) Utterson stops visiting Jekyll so often because:

Jekyll will never see him ☐   he does not like the gloomy atmosphere ☐
he would rather talk to Poole ☐

THINKING MORE DEEPLY ❓

❷ Write **one** or **two sentences** in response to each of these questions:

a) How does Utterson explain the change in Lanyon to himself?

b) What does Jekyll tell Utterson in his letter?

c) How does Stevenson present the death of Lanyon?

EXAM PREPARATION: WRITING ABOUT MYSTERY

Reread the passage from *'As soon as he got home'* to *'some deeper ground'* (p. 32).

Question: How does Stevenson build a sense of mystery in Jekyll's letter to Utterson?

Think about:

- What the letter says and does not say
- How it is presented

③ Complete this table:

Point/detail	Evidence	Effect or explanation
1: *Stevenson directs us to feel sympathy for Jekyll and find mystery in the letter.*	*'very pathetically worded, and sometimes darkly mysterious'*	*Stevenson alerts us to look out for mystery – for what is left unsaid in the letter. He also encourages us to feel pity for Jekyll, noting that the letter is 'pathetically worded'.*
2: *Jekyll sets out his desire to be alone and says he will not give his reasons for it.*		
3: *Jekyll speaks extravagantly of the horror of his situation, but gives no details.*		

④ Write up **point 1** into a **paragraph** below in your own words. Remember to include what you infer from the evidence, or the writer's effects:

....

....

....

....

....

⑤ Now, choose one of your **other points** and write it out as another **paragraph** here:

....

....

....

....

....

....

PROGRESS LOG [tick the correct box]   Needs more work ☐   Getting there ☐   Under control ☐

Chapter Seven: Incident at the Window

QUICK TEST ✔

❶ Complete this **gap-fill paragraph** about the chapter, with the **correct or suitable information**:

Utterson is walking with Enfield, his ...., when they come to the same door as they saw in their walk in Chapter One. Now, Enfield has discovered that the door is a back .... to Jekyll's property and is .... that he did not know it sooner. Jekyll is sitting at the window, but looks pale and .... He refuses to come out for a walk with them because he is .... While he is prepared to talk at the window, a look of .... crosses his face and he withdraws quickly. Utterson and Enfield are ....

THINKING MORE DEEPLY ?

❷ Write **one** or **two sentences** in response to each of these questions:

a) Why does Stevenson say that Jekyll is like 'some disconsolate prisoner' (p. 34)?

....

....

....

....

....

b) What does Stevenson tells us about the time of day that Enfield and Utterson take their walk?

....

....

....

....

c) Why does Utterson say 'God forgive us, God forgive us' (p. 35)?

....

....

....

....

EXAM PREPARATION: WRITING ABOUT MOOD

Reread the passage from *'What! Jekyll!'* (p. 34) to *'"God forgive us," said Mr Utterson'* (p. 35).

Question: What effect does Stevenson create with this encounter between Jekyll, Utterson and Enfield?

Think about:

- How the mood changes
- How Stevenson conveys the change in mood

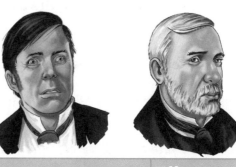

③ Complete this table:

Point/detail	Evidence	Effect or explanation
1: *At first, Utterson tries to cheer Jekyll up, being jolly and encouraging.*	*'"You stay too much indoors," said the lawyer.'*	*Utterson is treating Jekyll's low mood lightly, suggesting that fresh air will make him feel better.*
2: *Jekyll introduces a hint of mystery in his refusal to leave his room, saying he is afraid to.*		
3: *Stevenson quickly switches from a light tone to terror, as shown in the change in Jekyll's face.*		

④ Write up **point 1** into a **paragraph** below in your own words. Remember to include what you infer from the evidence, or the writer's effects:

....

....

....

....

⑤ Now, choose one of your **other points** and write it out as another **paragraph** here:

....

....

....

....

PROGRESS LOG [tick the correct box]   Needs more work ☐   Getting there ☐   Under control ☐

Chapter Eight: The Last Night

QUICK TEST ✔

❶ Who is each character talking **about** or **to**? **Write a name** from the list below next to **each quotation**.

Utterson   Jekyll   Poole   Bradshaw   Hyde   the maid   Messrs Maw

a) Utterson: 'you and <u>the boy</u> must go around the corner with a pair of good sticks' (p. 43) ....

b) Narrator: '<u>his</u> face was white and his voice, when he spoke, harsh and broken.' (p. 37) ....

c) Poole: 'Hold <u>your</u> tongue!' (p. 38) ....

d) Jekyll [letter]: 'He assures <u>them</u> that their last sample is impure' (p. 40) ....

e) Hyde: 'Tell <u>him</u> I cannot see anyone' (p. 38) ....

f) Poole: '<u>he</u> was made away with, eight days ago' (p. 39) ....

g) Poole: 'there was something queer about <u>that gentleman</u>' (p. 42) ....

THINKING MORE DEEPLY ?

❷ Write **one** or **two sentences** in response to each of these questions:

a) Why does Utterson decide that Hyde has killed himself?

....

....

....

....

b) Why is Utterson irritated to find all the servants standing around the fire at Jekyll's house?

....

....

....

c) How does Stevenson present Jekyll's cabinet as Utterson and Poole break down the door?

....

....

....

EXAM PREPARATION: WRITING ABOUT SUSPENSE

Reread the passage from '"Seen him?" repeated Mr Utterson' (p. 40) to 'there was murder done' (p. 41).

Question: How does Stevenson keep his readers guessing in this passage?

Think about:

- What is said
- Possible explanations

③ Complete this table:

Point/detail	Evidence	Effect or explanation
1: *Poole presents the mystery of who is in the cabinet by pointing out all that is odd.*	*'if that was my master, why had he a mask upon his face?'*	*Stevenson increases the sense of mystery by presenting facts in the form of questions.*
2: *Utterson gives an explanation that seems to remove the mystery.*		
3: *Poole reveals the man's height last; it demolishes Utterson's explanation.*		

④ Write up **point 1** into a **paragraph** below in your own words. Remember to include what you infer from the evidence, or the writer's effects:

....

....

....

....

⑤ Now, choose one of your **other points** and write it out as another **paragraph** here:

....

....

....

....

....

PROGRESS LOG [tick the correct box]   Needs more work ☐   Getting there ☐   Under control ☐

Chapter Nine: Dr Lanyon's Narrative

QUICK TEST ✔

❶ Which of these are **True** statements about this chapter, and which are **False**?
Write **'T'** or **'F'** in the boxes:

a) Jekyll wants Lanyon to bring the contents of the drawer to him. ☐

b) Lanyon suspects that Jekyll has something wrong with his mind. ☐

c) The door to Jekyll's cabinet is broken down. ☐

d) Jekyll's potion is made from a white powder and a red liquid. ☐

e) Hyde mixes the potion in front of Lanyon. ☐

f) Hyde persuades Lanyon to watch the transformation. ☐

g) Lanyon knows that what he has seen will kill him. ☐

THINKING MORE DEEPLY ?

❷ Write **one** or **two sentences** in response to each of these questions:

a) Why is Lanyon surprised to receive a letter from Jekyll?

....

....

....

....

....

....

b) Why does Lanyon load his gun while waiting for Jekyll's messenger?

....

....

....

....

....

....

c) What is laughable about Hyde's clothing?

....

....

....

....

....

....

EXAM PREPARATION: WRITING ABOUT SCIENCE	A03

Reread the passage from *'Have you a graduated glass?'* (p. 54) to *'with an air of scrutiny'* (p. 55).

Question: How does Stevenson show Lanyon's and Hyde's attitudes towards science in this passage?

Think about:

● What happens

● How Lanyon and Hyde describe it

③ Complete this table:

Point/detail	Evidence	Effect or explanation
1: *Stevenson makes Lanyon give a very precise description of the potion.*	*'began … to effervesce audibly, and to throw off small fumes of vapour.'*	*This suits Lanyon's character as a practical scientist – he tries to give a detailed account of what he observes.*
2: *Hyde suggests that scientific knowledge can bring power.*		
3: *Hyde uses wording that sounds like an ominous threat.*		

④ Write up **point 1** into a **paragraph** below in your own words. Remember to include what you infer from the evidence, or the writer's effects:

....

....

....

....

....

⑤ Now, choose one of your **other points** and write it out as another **paragraph** here:

....

....

....

....

....

| **PROGRESS LOG** [tick the correct box] | Needs more work ☐ | Getting there ☐ | Under control ☐ |

Chapter Ten: Henry Jekyll's Full Statement of the Case

QUICK TEST ✔

❶ Complete this **gap-fill paragraph** about the chapter, with the **correct or suitable information**:

Jekyll tried to protect himself from discovery by renting rooms for Hyde in

............................., employing a .... who would keep quiet and not

complain about his behaviour. Jekyll also told his own .... that

Hyde would be coming and going, and made a point of .... his

own house as Hyde so that they knew him. Jekyll made out his ....

in favour of Hyde and gave it to .... so that Hyde could still use his

money if Jekyll ....

❷ Choose the **correct answer** to finish the statement and **tick the box**:

a) Jekyll is driven to split his personality because he:

wants to commit evil acts ☐   wants to appear upright and proper ☐
is curious to see whether he can do it ☐

b) When Jekyll first took his potion he felt:

terrible pain and sickness ☐   a thrilling feeling ☐   lightheaded ☐

c) Jekyll realises that he has changed into Hyde in his sleep because he:

sees his reflection ☐   is in the wrong room ☐   sees his hand ☐

d) Jekyll decides to stop using his potion after:

Hyde tramples over a small girl ☐   Hyde kills Carew ☐
having to send Lanyon to fetch his chemicals ☐

e) Jekyll could make no more potion because he:

had run out of red liquid ☐   could not get the right white powder ☐
could not go to the chemist as Hyde ☐

THINKING MORE DEEPLY

❸ Write **one** or **two sentences** in response to each of these questions:

a) Jekyll is the only person not repelled by the sight of Hyde. Why?

....

....

....

....

b) Why is Jekyll so terrified to find that he changes into Hyde without taking the potion?

....

....

....

....

c) Why does Jekyll say the 'true hour' of his death is approaching at the end of his statement?

....

....

....

....

d) Why does Hyde send Lanyon to get the drawer of chemicals instead of going himself?

....

....

....

....

e) Why does Jekyll try so hard not to sleep?

....

....

....

....

f) Why does Hyde destroy Jekyll's precious belongings?

....

....

....

....

EXAM PREPARATION: WRITING ABOUT TRANSFORMATION   A02

Reread the passage from *'The most racking pangs'* (p. 59) to *'the appearance of Edward Hyde'* (p. 60).

Question: How does Stevenson present the transformation in this passage?

Think about:

- How the transformation is described
- How Jekyll feels

④ Complete this table:

Point/detail	Evidence	Effect or explanation
1: Jekyll experiences terror at the moment of transformation.	'a horror of the spirit that cannot be exceeded at the hour of birth or death.'	The experience is the equivalent of both a birth (of Hyde) and a death (of Jekyll).
2: Jekyll is thrilled to feel his new, evil self.		
3: Stevenson stresses the novelty of the released Hyde.		

⑤ Write up **point 1** into a **paragraph** below in your own words. Remember to include what you infer from the evidence, or the writer's effects:

....

....

....

....

⑥ Now, choose one of your **other points** and write it out as another **paragraph** here:

....

....

....

....

....

PROGRESS LOG [tick the correct box]   Needs more work ☐   Getting there ☐   Under control ☐

Reread the passage from *'But when I slept'* (p. 72) to *'with which he was himself regarded'* (p. 73).

Question: How does Stevenson use language and style to communicate Jekyll's feelings?

Think about:

● The language and imagery used

● Their effects

7 Complete this table:

Point/detail	Evidence	Effect or explanation
1: *Jekyll's account switches from the first person ('I') to third person, talking about both Jekyll and Hyde as others.*	*'The powers of Hyde seemed to have grown with the sickliness of Jekyll.'*	*In this way Stevenson shows that Jekyll has lost track of himself, no longer knowing which identity the pronoun 'I' relates to.*
2: *Jekyll's account of his feelings about Hyde is full of vivid, physical imagery.*		
3: *Jekyll describes Hyde in terms of things not living ('inorganic') but that act as if alive.*		

8 Write up **point 1** into a **paragraph** below in your own words. Remember to include what you infer from the evidence, or the writer's effects:

....

....

....

....

9 Now, choose one of your **other points** and write it out as another **paragraph** here:

....

....

....

....

....

PROGRESS LOG [tick the correct box]   Needs more work ☐   Getting there ☐   Under control ☐

Practice task

1 First, **read** this **exam-style** task:

> After a period of apparent normality, Jekyll has refused to see Utterson. Utterson visits Lanyon to ask if he knows why.
>
> Read from: *'The fifth night, he had in Guest to dine with him'* to *'any allusion to one whom I regard as dead'* (p. 31).
>
> Question: How does Stevenson create mystery and suspense in this extract?

2 Begin by circling the **key words** in the **question** above.

3 Now complete this table, noting down **three or four key points** with **evidence** and the **effect created**.

Point	Evidence/quotation	Effect or explanation

4 **Draft your response**. Use the space below for your first paragraph(s) and then continue on a sheet of paper.

Start: *In this extract, Stevenson builds up mystery about Lanyon's state of health and what has caused it. Firstly, he ...*

....

....

....

....

....

....

PROGRESS LOG [tick the correct box]   Needs more work ☐   Getting there ☐   Under control ☐

PART THREE: Characters

Who's who?

Look at these drawings and **complete** the **name(s)** of each of the characters shown.

Dr ....

Doctor

Mr ....

Lawyer

Dr ....

Mr ....

....

Dr Jekyll's butler

Inspector ....

Dr Henry Jekyll

❶ Look at these statements about Dr Jekyll. For each one, decide whether it is **True [T]**, **False [F]** or whether there is **Not Enough Evidence [NEE]** to make a decision.

a) Jekyll likes drinking and partying with women.   [T] [F] [NEE]

b) Jekyll has known Dr Lanyon since his schooldays.   [T] [F] [NEE]

c) Jekyll lives in a large house in Cavendish Square.   [T] [F] [NEE]

d) Jekyll was living a double life even before making his potion.   [T] [F] [NEE]

e) Jekyll is afraid that Hyde will kill himself.   [T] [F] [NEE]

f) Jekyll is trained in medicine.   [T] [F] [NEE]

g) Jekyll is older than Utterson.   [T] [F] [NEE]

❷ Complete these sentences about Henry Jekyll:

a) From early in his career, Jekyll wanted to be seen as ....
....
....

b) Dr Lanyon considers Jekyll to be ....
....
....

c) Mr Utterson worries that Jekyll is being ....
....
....

d) Jekyll is horrified at the prospect of ....
....
....

e) Jekyll's attitude to upsetting Lanyon by allowing him to witness the
transformation is ....
....
....

❸ Using your own judgement, put a mark along this line to show Robert Louis Stevenson's overall presentation of Dr Henry Jekyll:

Not at all sympathetic	A little sympathetic	Quite sympathetic	Very sympathetic
①	②	③	④

PROGRESS LOG [tick the correct box]   Needs more work ☐   Getting there ☐   Under control ☐

Mr Edward Hyde

❶ Look at the bank of **adjectives** describing Mr Hyde. Circle those you think best **describe** him:

repellent	fiendish	scheming	disturbed
unfeeling	energetic	violent	pleasure-seeking
joyful shy	cruel	manipulative	uncontrolled
stupid	cowardly	life-loving	secretive

❷ Now add a **page reference** from your copy of the novella next to each circle, showing where evidence can be found to **support** the **adjective**.

❸ Complete this **gap-fill paragraph** about Hyde, with the **correct or suitable information**:

Mr Hyde is a manifestation of the .... aspects of Dr Jekyll's

character, appearing when Jekyll takes a .... He is not a normal

human character. Jekyll describes him as being pure .... He thinks

only of his own ...., carrying out acts of .... without

.... for others. He becomes .... the more Jekyll takes

the potion, and his behaviour grows .... Everyone who sees him

finds him instantly and strangely ....

❹ Using your own judgement, put a mark along this line to show Robert Louis Stevenson's overall presentation of Mr Hyde:

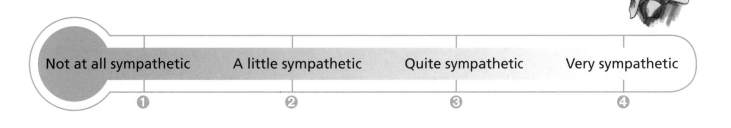

Not at all sympathetic   A little sympathetic   Quite sympathetic   Very sympathetic

❶   ❷   ❸   ❹

PROGRESS LOG [tick the correct box]   Needs more work ☐   Getting there ☐   Under control ☐

Mr Gabriel John Utterson

❶ Each of the character traits below could be applied to Mr Utterson. Working from **memory**, add evidence from the novella showing how or when you think these are shown, then find at least one **quotation** to back up each idea.

Quality	Evidence	Quotation(s)
a) Level-headed		
b) Well-liked		
c) Non-judgemental		
e) Jumps to conclusions		

❷ Look at this quotation about Utterson setting Lanyon's letter aside. Add further annotations to it by finding suitable adjectives from the bank at the bottom of the page and explaining how Stevenson's words help to convey Utterson's character.

'A great curiosity came on the trustee, to disregard the prohibition and dive at once to the bottom of these mysteries; but honour and faith to his dead friend were stringent obligations; and the packet slept in the inmost corner of his private safe.' (p. 33)

professional – his job as lawyer demands that he subdue his curiosity

professional	*impetuous*	*bored*	*self-controlled*	*unconcerned*
prying	*loyal*	*mean*	*callous*	*uninterested*	*lazy*

PROGRESS LOG [tick the correct box]   Needs more work ☐   Getting there ☐   Under control ☐

Dr Hastie Lanyon

❶ Without checking the book, write down from memory at least **two pieces of information** we are told about Dr Lanyon in each of these areas:

His manner and appearance before his shock	1.
	2.
His attitude towards science	1.
	2.
His social position	1.
	2.

❷ Now **check your facts**. Are you right? Look at the following pages:

  a) His manner and appearance before his shock: p. 9

  b) His attitude towards science: p.10

  c) His social position: p. 9

❸ Complete this **gap-fill paragraph** about Dr Lanyon, with the **correct or suitable information**:

Dr Lanyon was originally good .... with Jekyll, but disagreed with

his approach to .... He considered Jekyll's approach too

............................, but never imagined what Jekyll had succeeded in doing. When

he witnesses Jekyll's .... into Hyde after mixing his

............................, Lanyon's worldview is so .... he finds life

.... Re-evaluating his view of what is .... is too much

for him, and the shock kills him.

PROGRESS LOG [tick the correct box]   Needs more work ☐   Getting there ☐   Under control ☐

Mr Richard Enfield

❶ Look at the bank of **adjectives** describing Mr Enfield. Circle those you think best **describe** him:

proud	*confident*	*just*	*sociable*
fashionable	*cautious*	*shy*	*observant*
popular	*vindictive*	*active*	*prim*
friendly	*judgemental*	*talkative*	*callous*

❷ Now add a **page reference** from your copy of the novella next to each circle, showing where evidence can be found to **support** the **adjective**.

❸ Complete this **gap-fill paragraph** about Mr Enfield, with the **correct or suitable information**:

Enfield is Utterson's .... The pair take regular .... together, which they mostly pass in .... People are surprised at their friendship as they are quite unlike each other, Utterson being quiet and sober while Enfield is considered a 'man about ....'. In his dealings with .... he shows himself to be .... and forceful. He is active in pursuing .... in the form of compensation for the young girl's family.

❹ Using your own judgement, put a mark along this line to show Robert Louis Stevenson's overall presentation of Mr Enfield:

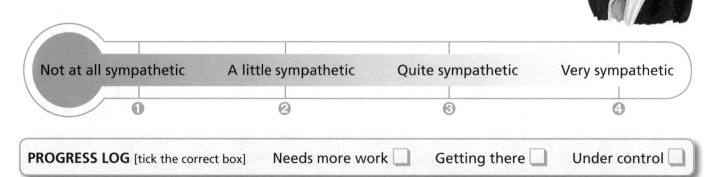

Not at all sympathetic	A little sympathetic	Quite sympathetic	Very sympathetic
❶	❷	❸	❹

PROGRESS LOG [tick the correct box]   Needs more work ☐   Getting there ☐   Under control ☐

Poole

❶ Each of the character traits below could be applied to Poole. Working from **memory**, add points in the novella when you think these are shown, then find at least one **quotation** to back up each idea.

Quality	Evidence	Quotation(s)
a) Loyal		
b) Resourceful		
c) Articulate		
d) Compassionate		

❷ Look at this quotation from Poole. Add further annotations to it by finding suitable adjectives from the bank at the bottom of the page and explaining how Stevenson's words help to convey Poole's character.

'Well, when that masked thing like a monkey jumped from among the chemicals and whipped into the cabinet, it went down my spine like ice. 'O, I know it's not evidence Mr Utterson; I'm book-learned enough for that; but a man has his feelings, and I give you my bible-word it was Mr Hyde!' (p.42)

partly educated – he knows enough to recognise a feeling is not legal evidence

embarrassed	honest	frightened	cowardly	scornful
Christian	superstitious	articulate	crazed	educated

PROGRESS LOG [tick the correct box]   Needs more work ☐   Getting there ☐   Under control ☐

Mr Guest

❶ Look at these statements about Mr Guest. For each one, decide whether it is **True [T]**, **False [F]** or whether there is **Not Enough Evidence [NEE]** to make a decision.

a) Guest decides from his handwriting that Hyde is unstable.   [T] [F] [NEE]

b) Guest is a close friend of Mr Utterson.   [T] [F] [NEE]

c) Guest is an expert in reading character from handwriting.   [T] [F] [NEE]

d) Guest does not drink alcohol.   [T] [F] [NEE]

e) Guest is very superstitious.   [T] [F] [NEE]

f) Utterson trusts Guest's judgement.   [T] [F] [NEE]

g) Guest is always slow to give his opinion on any matter.   [T] [F] [NEE]

❷ Complete these statements about Guest:

a) Guest works for Mr Utterson as

b) Guest has frequently visited

c) Guest changes his view of Hyde's sanity after

d) Guest addresses Utterson as 'sir' because

e) Guest's role in the novella is

❸ Using your own judgement, annotate the image of Mr Guest with adjectives to describe him. Then put a mark along the line to show Robert Louis Stevenson's overall presentation of Mr Guest:

skilled

Not at all sympathetic	A little sympathetic	Quite sympathetic	Very sympathetic
❶	❷	❸	❹

PROGRESS LOG [tick the correct box]   Needs more work ☐   Getting there ☐   Under control ☐

Inspector Newcomen and Sir Danvers Carew

1 Each of the character traits below could be applied to **Inspector Newcomen**. Working from **memory**, add points in the novella when you think these are shown, then find at least one **quotation** to back up each idea.

Quality	Evidence	Quotation(s)
a) Ambitious		
b) Confident		
c) Uneducated		
d) Efficient		

2 Complete this **gap-fill paragraph** about **Sir Danvers Carew**, with the **correct or suitable information**:

Sir Danvers Carew is seen only by the maid and described in the novella after his

.... The maid says he is old and .... From the

way he behaves, he seems to be very .... He was a friend and

.... of Utterson, and Utterson has a .... opinion of

him. As we trust Utterson's judgement, we are likely to accept this as ....

.... Carew worked as an ...., so we would expect him to be

....

3 Using your own judgement, put a mark along this line to show Robert Louis Stevenson's overall presentation of Sir Danvers Carew:

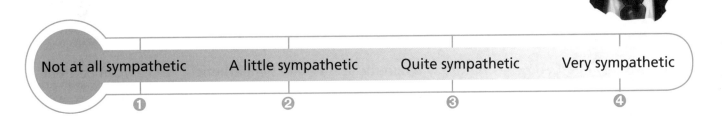

Not at all sympathetic	A little sympathetic	Quite sympathetic	Very sympathetic
1	2	3	4

PROGRESS LOG [tick the correct box]   Needs more work ☐   Getting there ☐   Under control ☐

The maid and Hyde's landlady

❶ Look at these statements about **the maid**. For each one, decide whether it is
True [T], **False [F]** or whether there is **Not Enough Evidence [NEE]**
to make a decision.

a) The maid lives alone.   [T] [F] [NEE]

b) She recognises Carew as she knows him.   [T] [F] [NEE]

c) She was upset by what she saw and the distress stayed with her.   [T] [F] [NEE]

d) Her account of the murder suggests she is romantic
   and imaginative.   [T] [F] [NEE]

e) She is harsh and unsympathetic.   [T] [F] [NEE]

f) She finds Carew appealing.   [T] [F] [NEE]

g) She is highly strung and unreliable as a witness.   [T] [F] [NEE]

❷ Complete these statements about **the landlady**:

a) The landlady has a pale face and ....

....

b) The narrator suggests she is ....

....

....

c) She seems pleased to learn that ....

....

....

d) Jekyll employed her because she would keep quiet and ....

....

....

e) The landlady's manners are ....

....

....

❸ Using your own judgement, put a mark along this line
to show Robert Louis Stevenson's overall presentation
of the landlady:

Not at all sympathetic	A little sympathetic	Quite sympathetic	Very sympathetic
❶	❷	❸	❹

PROGRESS LOG [tick the correct box]   Needs more work ☐   Getting there ☐   Under control ☐

Practice task

❶ First, **read** this **exam-style** task:

What do we learn of Dr Jekyll's character, both in the past and in the period of time covered by the action of the novella?

❷ Begin by circling the **key words** in the **question** above.

❸ Now complete this table, noting down **three or four key points** with **evidence** and the **effect created**.

Point	Evidence/quotation	Effect or explanation

❹ **Draft your response**. Use the space below for your first paragraph(s) and then continue on a sheet of paper.

Start: *We are shown Jekyll's character in the period covered by the action of the story, and also given an insight into his past through his statement. He appears …*

PROGRESS LOG [tick the correct box]   Needs more work ☐   Getting there ☐   Under control ☐

PART FOUR: THEMES, CONTEXTS AND SETTINGS

Themes

❶ Complete this **gap-fill paragraph** about the theme of social position, with the **correct or suitable information**:

> *Robert Louis Stevenson often draws attention to social position and*
>
> *............................. . Jekyll says he was concerned to appear ....*
>
> *and was .... of his pleasures. Hyde is willing to pay money to the*
>
> *girl's family because he is keen to avoid a .... Utterson is sharp*
>
> *with Jekyll's servants for standing around together on the last night as he*
>
> *considers it .... and unseemly. Poole addresses Mr Utterson*
>
> *as '.............................' but Utterson calls him 'Poole' because he considers himself*
>
> *Poole's social ....*

❷ These comments by different characters suggest a particular theme in the novella. From the list below, choose the best **abstract noun or phrase** to identify the **theme** in each comment.

a) Dr Lanyon: 'I continue to take an interest in him for old sake's sake' **(p. 9)**

....

b) Poole: 'It was for but one minute that I saw him, but the hair stood upon my head like quills.' **(p.40)**

....

c) Utterson: 'now I begin to fear it is disgrace.' **(p. 9)**

....

d) Jekyll: 'I only ask for justice' **(p. 19)**

....

e) Hyde: 'Have you a graduated glass?' **(p. 54)**

....

social standing	*good and evil*	*duality*
science	*law*	*transformation*
natural and unnatural		*friendship*

THINKING MORE DEEPLY

❸ Complete each **statement** about the theme of **duality**.

a) The main focus of duality is on the two aspects of human nature. These are explored through …

....

....

b) There are many examples of events having a dual aspect, of things seeming to be one way and actually being another, such as …

....

....

....

c) Jekyll's own house has a dual character, with …

....

....

....

d) Even before he started to take his potion, Jekyll felt he lived a double life because …

....

....

....

❹ Write **two** or **three sentences** to show how quotations a) and b) in Question 2 reveal their **themes**. Include a comment on the writer's effects.

a) Dr Lanyon's comment raises the theme of:

....

....

....

Stevenson shows: ....

....

....

b) Poole's response to seeing Hyde briefly relates to the theme of:

....

....

....

Stevenson's effect: ....

....

⑤ Write **one** or **two sentences** in response to each of these questions about the themes of the novella. Include a comment on the writer's effects.

a) Which theme do we associate with Utterson, and how does Stevenson present it through him?

....

....

....

....

b) How does Stevenson use language to emphasise the theme of good and evil?

....

....

....

....

c) How does Stevenson explore two themes, duality and science, in Jekyll and Lanyon?

....

....

....

....

⑥ Write **one** or **two sentences** to show how these comments reveal the character's attitude to the theme of science.

a) Lanyon: 'The mixture, which was at first of a reddish hue, began, in proportion as the crystals melted, to brighten in colour, to effervesce audibly, and to throw off small fumes.' **(p. 55)**

....

....

....

....

b) Jekyll: 'the direction of my scientific studies, which led wholly towards the mystic and the transcendental' **(pp. 57–58)**

....

....

....

....

c) Poole: 'Every time I brought the stuff back there would be another paper telling me to return it, because it was not pure' **(p. 39)**

....

....

....

....

EXAM PREPARATION: WRITING ABOUT UNNATURALNESS

EXAM PREPARATION: WRITING ABOUT UNNATURALNESS

Reread the passage from *'The lawyer stood a while'* (p. 13) to *'your new friend'* (p. 14).

Question: How does Stevenson communicate the unnaturalness of Hyde?

Think about:

● How Utterson feels about Hyde

● The words used to describe Hyde

7 Complete this table:

Point/detail	Evidence	Effect or explanation
1: Utterson feels instantly repelled by Hyde.	*'the hitherto unknown disgust, loathing and fear with which Mr Utterson regarded him'*	*Disgust, loathing and fear are strong responses, and have more impact because Utterson is a mild man.*
3: Utterson finds something subhuman about Hyde.		
3 Hyde is linked with the Devil by the language Stevenson uses.		

8 Write up **point 1** into a **paragraph** below in your own words. Remember to include what you infer from the evidence, or the writer's effects:

....

....

....

....

....

9 Now, choose one of your **other points** and write it out as another **paragraph** here:

....

....

....

....

....

....

PROGRESS LOG [tick the correct box]   Needs more work ☐   Getting there ☐   Under control ☐

Contexts

QUICK TEST ✔

❶ Choose the **correct answer** about the context of the novella to finish the statement and **tick the box**:

a) The weather most frequently mentioned in the novella is:
rain ☐   snow ☐   fog ☐

b) The action of the novella takes place in:
London ☐   Edinburgh ☐   Liverpool ☐

c) The novella is most closely related to the genre of:
romance ☐   Gothic fiction ☐   detective fiction ☐

d) The novella is set in: the Victorian age ☐
the eighteenth century ☐   the early nineteenth century ☐

e) Science was of interest to Stevenson's readers because of:
its complete novelty ☐   recent scientific developments ☐
recent scandals involving scientists ☐

f) Robert Louis Stevenson was trained as:
a doctor ☐   a lawyer ☐   an engineer ☐

THINKING MORE DEEPLY ❓

❷ Write **one** or **two sentences** in response to each of these questions:

a) How is Darwin's theory of evolution relevant to *Dr Jekyll and Mr Hyde*?

....

....

....

....

b) Why does Utterson show Guest the letter that Jekyll says came from Hyde?

....

....

....

....

....

c) How are the law and the legal profession important in the novella?

....

....

....

....

....

EXAM PREPARATION: WRITING ABOUT GOTHIC TRADITION (A03)

Reread the passage from: *'The most racking pangs succeeded'* (p. 59) to *'I had lost in stature'* (p. 60).

Question: How does Stevenson make use of the Gothic tradition in this extract?

③ Complete this table:

Point/detail	Evidence	Effect or explanation
1: *Stevenson uses vivid, flamboyant language.*	*'a grinding in the bones, deadly nausea, and a horror of the spirit'*	*Extreme and extravagant language is a common feature of Gothic literature, and is designed to inspire horror in the reader.*
2: *Events seem to be unnatural or supernatural.*		
3: *Stevenson creates a sense of shock by showing Jekyll delighting in recognising his evil.*		

④ Write up **point 1** into a **paragraph** below in your own words. Remember to include what you infer from the evidence, or the writer's effects:

....

....

....

....

....

....

⑤ Now, choose one of your **other points** and write it out as another **paragraph** here:

....

....

....

....

....

....

....

PROGRESS LOG [tick the correct box]   Needs more work ☐   Getting there ☐   Under control ☐

Settings

❶ Write the key events linked to each location. For example, you could write: 'where Hyde went in to fetch a cheque the night he trampled over the young girl' beside Jekyll's house – back.

Dr Jekyll's house – front

Dr Jekyll's house – back

Events:

....

....

....

....

Events:

....

....

....

....

Mr Utterson's house

Dr Lanyon's house

Mr Hyde's lodgings

Events:

....

....

....

....

Events:

....

....

....

....

Events:

....

....

....

....

THINKING MORE DEEPLY

❷ Write **one** or **two sentences** in response to each of these questions about the settings of the novella. Include a comment on the writer's effects.

a) Where is the novella set? Why do you think Stevenson set it here?

....

....

....

....

b) How does the weather contribute to the atmosphere of the setting?

....

....

....

....

c) How does Stevenson achieve the effect of Jekyll's house having two contrasting aspects?

....

....

....

....

❸ Complete these sentences about **important locations** in the novella.

a) To get from Jekyll's house to his cabinet, it is necessary to …

....

....

....

b) On the last night, Jekyll's cabinet has contrasting elements. It has …

....

....

....

....

c) Hyde's rooms also have a dual aspect, which Stevenson presents by showing …

....

....

....

....

PROGRESS LOG [tick the correct box]   Needs more work ☐   Getting there ☐   Under control ☐

Practice task

❶ First, **read** this **exam-style** task:

Question: Stevenson explores the theme of duality in different ways in *The Strange Case of Dr Jekyll and Mr Hyde*. Describe two areas in which he shows dual aspects and how he creates this effect.

❷ Begin by circling the **key words** in the **question** above.

❸ Now complete this table, noting down **three or four key points** with **evidence** and the **effect created**.

Point	Evidence/quotation	Effect or explanation

❹ **Draft your response.** Use the space below for your first paragraph(s) and then continue on a sheet of paper.

Start: *I will focus on how duality is presented in these aspects of the novella:* ....

....

....

....

....

....

....

....

....

....

....

....

PROGRESS LOG [tick the correct box]   Needs more work ☐   Getting there ☐   Under control ☐

PART FIVE: FORM, STRUCTURE AND LANGUAGE

Form

QUICK TEST

1 Choose the **correct answer** about the form of the novella to finish the statement and **tick the box**.

a) The novella is related by: a third-person narrator ☐
   a first-person narrator ☐   several narrators ☐

b) A novella is a story that: is shorter than a novel ☐
   has fewer than six characters ☐   never has female characters ☐

c) *Dr Jekyll and Mr Hyde* is told in: the order events happen ☐
   the order Utterson learns about events ☐   a jumbled sequence ☐

d) Letters, written statements and other characters' reports presented
   in a story are called: distraction narratives ☐
   interpolated narratives ☐   diversions ☐

e) In *Dr Jekyll and Mr Hyde*, we see some events before:
   understanding them ☐   they have happened ☐
   Utterson knows about them ☐

THINKING MORE DEEPLY

2 Write **one** or **two sentences** in response to each of these questions.

a) Which features of Gothic literature are apparent in *Dr Jekyll and Mr Hyde*?

....

....

....

....

b) How is *Dr Jekyll and Mr Hyde* like and unlike a detective story?

....

....

....

....

c) What does Stevenson achieve by using extra narratives such as
   Jekyll's statement and Lanyon's letter?

....

....

....

....

PROGRESS LOG [tick the correct box]   Needs more work ☐   Getting there ☐   Under control ☐

Structure

❶ Without checking the novella, try to remember in which chapter each of these scenes takes place:

Scene	Chapter
a: *Sir Danvers Carew is murdered.*	
b: *Poole and Utterson break down a door.*	
c: *Utterson and Enfield take their second walk.*	
d: *Hyde tramples a small girl.*	
e: *Lanyon witnesses the action of the potion on Hyde.*	
f: *Utterson visits Lanyon and finds him unwell.*	

THINKING MORE DEEPLY

❷ Write **one** or **two sentences** in response to each of these questions about the structure and plot:

a) What effect does Stevenson achieve by narrating events out of order?

....

....

....

....

b) How does Stevenson use minor characters such as the maid and Hyde's landlady?

....

....

....

....

c) What effect does Stevenson achieve by using paired events, such as Utterson's two walks with Enfield, his two visits to Lanyon, and Hyde's two attacks?

....

....

....

....

EXAM PREPARATION: WRITING ABOUT SUSPENSE

Reread the passage in which Hyde drinks the potion in front of Dr Lanyon, from *'"It is well," replied my visitor'* (p. 55) to *'there stood Henry Jekyll!'* (p. 56).

Question: How does Stevenson build suspense and create a climax in this extract?

③ Complete this table:

Point/Detail	Evidence	Effect or explanation
1: *Stevenson introduces the idea that something shocking will happen.*	*'what follows is under the vows of your profession … behold!'*	*The word 'behold' is a command to watch, and is associated with wonderful sights.*
2: *The progress of the change is presented in detail, but without explanation.*		
3: *The important revelation comes right at the end of the paragraph.*		

④ Write up **point 1** into a **paragraph** below in your own words. Remember to include what you infer from the evidence, or the writer's effects:

....

....

....

....

....

⑤ Now, choose one of your **other points** and write it out as another **paragraph** here:

....

....

....

....

....

....

PROGRESS LOG [tick the correct box]   Needs more work ☐   Getting there ☐   Under control ☐

Language

❶ First match these words/expressions to their meanings without checking the text:

Word/expression	Meaning
a) 'penny number'	fire
b) 'juggernaut'	drop
c) 'bland'	pamphlet
d) 'conflagration'	filmy
e) 'countenance'	unremarkable
f) 'diaphonous'	face
g) 'minim'	chariot

❷ Now check the words in context. Look at the following pages. Do you want to change any of your answers?

a) p. 23 b) p. 3 c) p. 5 d) p. 22 e) p. 59 f) p. 37 g) p. 55

THINKING MORE DEEPLY

❸ For each of the feelings listed below, think of a moment in the novella when it is expressed. Find a **quotation** to back up each of your **examples**.

Feeling	Moment in the novella	Quotation
1: Horror	When Lanyon sees Hyde turn into Jekyll	
2: Curiosity		
3: Anxiety		

④ Read these comments made by Utterson on the night he and Poole break into Jekyll's cabinet in Chapter Eight. From the list below choose the **best adjective** to sum up the tone of each comment:

a) 'That won't hold water, it doesn't commend itself to reason.' (p. 39) ....

b) 'What, what? Are you all here?' (p. 38) ....

c) 'Pull yourself together, Bradshaw' (p. 42) ....

d) 'he must still be alive, he must have fled!' (p. 47) ....

furious	afraid	brisk	weary
disbelieving	horrified	hopeful	kind	irritated

⑤ Write a **sentence** to describe how Utterson's tone of voice towards Poole **changes** over the course of this chapter.

....

....

....

In the novella several **literary techniques** are used. Read the **definitions** of these literary techniques:

● **Personification**: talking about something non-human as though it were a person.

● **Imagery**: using one object or situation to help describe or evoke another.

● **Rhetorical question**: asking a question without expecting it to be answered in order to draw attention to something.

⑥ Complete the table below, identifying the techniques used in each example/quotation and giving the meaning or effect.

Example of quotation	Literary technique	Meaning/effect
'the animal within me licking the chops of memory' (p. 69)	Imagery	Stevenson makes the image of Hyde as an animal much more vivid by causing us to think of an animal licking around its mouth after eating.
'if that was my master, why had he a mask upon his face?' (p. 40)		
'these powers should be dethroned from their supremacy' (p. 59)		

EXAM PREPARATION: WRITING ABOUT THE EFFECTS OF LANGUAGE **A02**

Reread the passage in Jekyll's letter to Lanyon asking him to bring the drawer from his cabinet, from *'That is the first part of the service'* to *'save Your friend, H.J.'* (p. 50)

Question: What techniques does Stevenson use to show us Jekyll's frame of mind?

Think about:

- How he phrases the letter
- The effect he wants it to have on Lanyon

7 Complete this table:

Technique	Example	Effect
1: *Long, convoluted sentences*	*'You should be back, if you set out at once ...'*	*This follows Jekyll's train of thought, which is tortured, confused and anxious.*
2: *Metaphor*		
3: *Personal address*		

8 Write up **point 1** into a **paragraph** below in your own words. Remember to include what you infer from the evidence, or the writer's effects:

....

....

....

....

9 Now, choose one of your **other points** and write it out as another **paragraph** here:

....

....

....

....

....

| **PROGRESS LOG** [tick the correct box] | Needs more work ☐ | Getting there ☐ | Under control ☐ |

Practice task

❶ First, **read** this **exam-style** task:

Jekyll is describing in his statement the time when he decided not to take the potion again, but then his resolve weakened and he did take it.

Read from: *'Yes, I preferred the elderly and discontented doctor'* (p. 66) to *'he came out roaring.'* (p. 67)

Question: How does Stevenson communicate Jekyll's state of mind and feelings about what he has done? Comment on the effect of Stevenson's language choices.

❷ Begin by circling the **key words** in the **question** above.

❸ Now complete this table, noting down **three or four key points** with **evidence** and the **effect created**.

Point	Evidence/Quotation	Effect or explanation

❹ **Draft your response**. Use the space below for your first paragraph(s) and then continue on a sheet of paper.

Start: *In this extract, Stevenson presents Jekyll outlining both his lifestyles, evoking the pleasant aspects of each. Firstly, he …*

....

....

....

....

....

....

....

PROGRESS LOG [tick the correct box]   Needs more work ☐   Getting there ☐   Under control ☐

PART SIX: Progress Booster

Expressing and explaining ideas (A01) (A04)*

❶ How well can you express your ideas about *The Strange Case of Dr Jekyll and Mr Hyde*? Look at this grid and tick the level you think you are currently at:

Level	How you respond	What your writing skills are like	Tick
High	• You analyse the effect of specific words and phrases very closely (i.e. 'zooming in' on them and exploring their meaning). • You select quotations very carefully and you embed them fluently in your sentences. • You are persuasive and convincing in the points you make, often coming up with original ideas.	• You use a wide range of specialist terms (words like 'imagery'), excellent punctuation, accurate spelling, grammar, etc.	
Mid/ Good	• You analyse some parts of the text closely, but not all the time. • You support what you say with evidence and quotations, but sometimes your writing could be more fluent to read. • You make relevant comments on the text.	• You use a good range of specialist terms, generally accurate punctuation, usually accurate spelling, grammar, etc.	
Lower	• You comment on some words and phrases but often you do not develop your ideas. • You sometimes use quotations to back up what you say but they are not always well chosen. • You mention the effect of certain words and phrases but these are not always relevant to the task.	• You do not have a very wide range of specialist terms, but you have reasonably accurate spelling, punctuation and grammar.	

SELECTING AND USING QUOTATIONS

❷ Read these two samples from students' responses to a question about how Utterson is presented. Decide which of the three levels they fit best, i.e. **lower** (L), **mid** (M) or **high** (H).

Student A: *Stevenson shows Utterson as level-headed most of the time. But he also jumps to conclusions, and persuades himself that Jekyll is being blackmailed, thinking 'Ay, it must be that' (p. 15). Then he acts on his assumption without testing whether it is right, so we see him deciding to 'put [his] shoulder to the wheel' in sorting it out for Jekyll. We seem to hear Utterson's own words as he thinks, so we have direct insight into his character.*

Level? ☐   Why? ....

Student B: *Utterson is usually sensible and we trust him to do things right. But when he gets an idea in his head, for example that Jekyll is being blackmailed, he just assumes it's right and doesn't bother to think about it properly. He says 'it turns me cold to think of this creature' creeping around Jekyll's bedroom, which is something he has entirely made up himself and not actually seen.*

Level? ☐   Why? ....

*AO4 is assessed by OCR only.

ZOOMING IN – YOUR TURN!

Here is the first part of another student response. The student has picked a good quotation but he has not 'zoomed in' on any particular words or phrases:

When Guest has shown Utterson that Jekyll wrote the note he pretends came from Hyde, Utterson leaps to another conclusion, thinking 'What! … Henry Jekyll forge for a murderer!' and Stevenson tells us his 'blood ran cold'. This shows how he quickly accepts it as true.

❸ Pick out one of the **words** or **phrases** the student has quoted and write a further sentence to complete the explanation:

The word/phrase ' .... *' suggests that* ....

....

....

EXPLAINING IDEAS

You need to be precise about the way Stevenson gets ideas across. This can be done by varying your use of verbs (not just using 'says' or 'means').

❹ Read this paragraph from a **mid-level** response to a question about Lanyon's attitude towards Jekyll. Circle all the **verbs** that are repeated (not in the quotations):

Lanyon says that Jekyll is 'one whom I consider dead' which shows that he wants nothing more to do with him. He then says that 'Nothing can be done' to repair their friendship, which effectively says to Utterson that he must stop trying to help. Lanyon says to Utterson that he can stay if he is willing to talk about something else. This shows that he still likes Utterson.

❺ Now choose some of the words below to replace your circled ones:

suggests	*implies*	*tells*	*presents*
signals	*asserts*	*demonstrates*	
states	*reveals*	*conveys*	*makes clear*

❻ Rewrite your **high-level** version of the paragraph in full below. Remember to mention the author by name to show you understand he is **making choices** in how he presents characters, themes and events.

....

....

....

....

....

....

PROGRESS LOG [tick the correct box]   Needs more work ☐   Getting there ☐   Under control ☐

Making inferences and interpretations

WRITING ABOUT INFERENCES

You need to be able to show you can read between the lines, and make inferences, rather than just explain more explicit 'surface' meanings.

Here is an extract from one student's **high-level** response to a question about Dr Lanyon and his relationship with Dr Jekyll/Mr Hyde:

When Hyde comes to Dr Lanyon's consulting room to find the drawer of chemicals, he is at first too eager and impatiently puts his hand on Lanyon's arm. Lanyon is irritated, but with an effort remains polite. When he says to Hyde 'You forget that I have not yet had the pleasure of your acquaintance' he uses a stock polite phrase without meaning it. This suggests that Lanyon does not really think there will be any pleasure in knowing Hyde, and indeed in the same sentence mentions the 'horror' many feel in the presence of Hyde.

❶ Look at the response carefully.

- **Underline** the simple point which explains Dr Lanyon's attitude.

- **Circle** the sentence that develops the first point.

- **Highlight** the sentence that shows an inference and begins to explore wider interpretations.

INTERPRETING – YOUR TURN!

❷ Read the opening to this student response carefully and then **choose the sentence** from the list which shows **inference** and could lead to a **deeper interpretation**. Remember – interpreting is *not* guesswork!

In his final statement, Jekyll mentions the depraved acts Hyde has committed but does not go into details. When he says 'Henry Jekyll stood at times aghast before the acts of Edward Hyde', this suggests ...

a) *... he doesn't know what Hyde did.*

b) *... he is appalled by the terrible things Hyde has done.*

c) *... he is unwilling to accept responsibility for the acts he committed as Hyde.*

❸ Now complete this **paragraph** about Jekyll, adding your own final sentence which makes inferences or explores wider interpretations:

When Jekyll talks about his earlier life, he refers to 'such irregularities as I was guilty of' as being sufficiently minor that other people might have exaggerated them. He, though, was ashamed of them and hid them because of his 'imperious desire to carry [his] head high'. This suggests that ...

....

....

....

PROGRESS LOG [tick the correct box]   Needs more work ☐   Getting there ☐   Under control ☐

Writing about context

EXPLAINING CONTEXT

When you write about context you must make sure that what you write is relevant to the task.

Read this comment by a student about Poole:

Utterson treats Poole as a social inferior, even as he would treat his own servant. This is clear in the way Utterson calls him 'my good man' and is sharp with him when he sees that the letter to the pharmacist has been opened. It is immediately clear that when Poole turns up at Utterson's house there must be something very wrong – this is not something someone like Poole would do in the normal course of events at that time.

❶ Why is this an effective paragraph about context?

   a) Because it shows how servants were treated in the nineteenth century.

   b) Because it shows how Stevenson uses social position to guide our expectations in this part of the plot.

   c) Because it suggests Utterson is not very nice really, even though we have come to like him so far.

EXPLAINING – YOUR TURN!

❷ Now read this further paragraph, and complete it by choosing a suitable point related to context.

Victorian attitudes towards science were ambivalent. On the one hand, people were excited by new developments, but on the other hand some of these challenged or threatened the way people saw the world, and it made them uncomfortable. Stevenson reflects these attitudes in the novella, for example:

   a) *Dr Lanyon calls Dr Jekyll's scientific interests 'fanciful' because he doesn't approve of anything out of the ordinary.*

   b) *Mr Hyde taunts Dr Lanyon, saying 'you who have derided your superiors' because scientists thought they were better than other people in the nineteenth century.*

   c) *Dr Lanyon says that his life is 'shaken to its roots' by what he has seen, which is how many people felt about the way science had assaulted their long-held beliefs about the world.*

❸ Now, on a separate sheet of paper, write a paragraph about how Stevenson uses the famous London fogs of the late nineteenth century to help fix the novella in its Gothic context.

PROGRESS LOG [tick the correct box]   Needs more work ☐   Getting there ☐   Under control ☐

Structure and linking of paragraphs (A01)

Paragraphs need to demonstrate your points clearly by:

- Using topic sentences
- Focusing on key words from quotations
- Explaining their effect or meaning

❶ Read this model paragraph in which a student explains how Stevenson shows Hyde in relation to other people.

Stevenson never shows Hyde responding to other people in any way other than with self-interest. Jekyll says that 'Hyde was indifferent to Jekyll' (p. 66). In saying he was 'indifferent', Jekyll means that Hyde neither likes nor dislikes Jekyll, though he later becomes afraid that Jekyll might kill himself and so put an end to Hyde, which is another selfish motive.

Look at the response carefully.

- **Underline** the topic sentence which explains the main point about Hyde.
- **Circle** the word that is picked out from the quotation.
- **Highlight** or put a tick next to the part of the last sentence which explains the word.

❷ Now read this **paragraph** by a student who is explaining how Stevenson presents London as Mr Utterson travels to Hyde's lodgings:

Utterson catches glimpses of London when the fog lifts. He says it is 'like a district of some city in a nightmare' (p. 22). This tells us that Utterson sometimes has bad dreams in which he sees an unpleasant city.

Expert viewpoint: This paragraph is unclear. It does not begin with a topic sentence to explain how Stevenson presents London and doesn't zoom in on any key words that tell us what London is like.

Now **rewrite the paragraph**. Start with a **topic sentence**, and pick out a **key word or phrase** to **'zoom in'** on, then follow up with an explanation or interpretation.

Stevenson presents London …

It is equally important to make your sentences link together and your ideas follow on fluently from each other. You can do this by:

- Using a mixture of short and long sentences as appropriate
- Using words or phrases that help connect or develop ideas

③ Read this model paragraph by one student writing about Jekyll in relation to the theme of duality:

Jekyll says that he was already committed to 'a profound duplicity in life' but once he begins to take his potion he goes from duplicity to duality, living as two different people. At first, he sees Hyde as part of himself that has been freed to act independently. But soon the border between his identity and Hyde's becomes blurred. He can no longer control which form he takes and his real identity becomes lost. Stevenson shows this through having Jekyll refer to both Jekyll and Hyde in the third person in his statement, implying that Jekyll no longer identifies as himself, or 'I'.

Look at the response carefully.

- **Underline** the topic sentence which introduces the main idea.
- **Underline** the short sentence which signals a change in ideas.
- **Circle** any words or phrases that link ideas such as 'who', 'when', 'implying', 'which', etc.

④ Read this **paragraph** by another student also commenting on how Stevenson presents Dr Lanyon:

Stevenson shows us two images of Dr Lanyon. One comes before Lanyon's shock and one after it. In the first, he is described as red-faced, happy, boisterous, healthy and with white hair. He jumps from his chair and seizes Utterson's hands. The second time we see him he looks older, balder, pale and thinner. He looks as though he is dying and as though he has been terrified.

Expert viewpoint: The candidate has understood how Lanyon is depicted in both scenes. However, the paragraph is rather awkwardly written. It needs improving by linking the sentences with suitable phrases and joining words such as: 'where', 'in', 'which', 'who', 'suggesting' or 'implying'.

Rewrite the paragraph, **improving the style,** and also try to add a **concluding sentence** summing up what Stevenson is showing through the change in Dr Lanyon's appearance.

Start with the same topic sentence, but extend it:

Stevenson gives us a vivid picture of the change in Dr Lanyon … ....

....

....

....

....

....

....

....

....

....

| **PROGRESS LOG** [tick the correct box] | Needs more work ☐ | Getting there ☐ | Under control ☐ |

Writing skills (A01) (A04)*

Here are a number of key words you might use when writing in the exam:

Content and structure	Characters and style	Linguistic features
chapter	character	metaphor
scene	role	personification
quotation	narrator	juxtaposition
sequence	dramatic	imagery
dialogue	Gothic	repetition
climax	extravagant	symbol
event	evil	reflecting
development	repellent	narrative
description	sympathetic	

① Circle any you might find difficult to spell, and then use the 'Look, Say, Cover, Write, Check' method to learn them. This means: **look** at the word; **say** it out loud; then **cover** it up; **write** it out; uncover and **check** your spelling with the correct version.

② Create a **mnemonic** for five of your difficult spellings. For example:

Narrator: **n**early **a**ll **r**agged **r**avens **a**re **t**otally **o**riginal **r**eaders!

Or break the word down: NAR – RAT – OR!

a) ....

b) ....

c) ....

d) ....

e) ....

③ Circle any **incorrect spellings** in this paragraph and then rewrite it:

Jekyll finds accomodation for Hyde in a dimsal area of Soho wear no one will take much notice of him. His landlady is unscrupulus and Jekyl trusts her not to interfer in what Hide does there.

....

....

....

....

*AO4 is assessed by OCR only.

④ **Punctuation** can help make your meaning clear. Here is one response by a student commenting on Stevenson's depiction of the law in Dr Jekyll and Mr Hyde.
Check for correct use of:

- Apostrophes
- Speech marks for quotations and emphasis
- Full stops, commas and capital letters

Stevenson presents the law through two characters Mr Utterson and Inspector Newcomen. being a lawyer is Uttersons job so he is supposed to know and uphold the law this makes it surprising when he hints that he might look into Hydes past to see if he can find anything to blackmail him about saying he 'must have secrets of his own; black secrets by the look of him

Rewrite it **correctly** here:

....

....

....

....

....

⑤ It is better to use the **present tense** to describe what is happening in the novel.

Look at these two extracts. Which one uses tenses **consistently** and **accurately**?

Student A: *Stevenson uses the famous London fogs to add atmosphere to the novella. When Mr Utterson and Inspector Newcomen went to Hyde's lodgings the fog was thick, with breaks in a few places. In the gaps, Utterson can see what kind of streets they were passing through and the type of people who lived there.*

Student B: *Stevenson uses the famous London fogs to add atmosphere to the novella. When Mr Utterson and Inspector Newcomen go to Hyde's lodgings the fog is thick, with breaks in a few places. In the gaps, Utterson can see what kind of streets they are passing through and the type of people who live there.*

⑥ Now look at this further paragraph. **Underline** or **circle** all the **verbs** first.

Stevenson used very flamboyant language with lots of imagery in Jekyll's final statement. Jekyll was trying to get across very difficult, unfamiliar ideas that he knows people would struggle with. To make them clearer, he will use imagery that evokes pictures of things that were more familiar.

Now rewrite it using the **present tense** consistently:

....

....

....

....

....

PROGRESS LOG [tick the correct box]   Needs more work ☐   Getting there ☐   Under control ☐

Tackling exam tasks (A01) (A02)

DECODING QUESTIONS

It is important to be able to identify key words in exam tasks and then quickly generate some ideas.

❶ Read this task and notice how the key words have been underlined.

Question: How does <u>Stevenson use the structure</u> of the novella to <u>control suspense</u>?

Write about:

- The way the <u>novella is structured</u>, especially the <u>order in which events are narrated</u>
- How <u>Stevenson</u> <u>controls suspense</u> by <u>withholding or revealing information</u>

Now do the same with this task, i.e. underline the key words:

Question: How does Stevenson present contrasting ideas about science in the novella?

Write about:

- Different ideas about science that are shown
- How Stevenson shows them

GENERATING IDEAS

❷ Now you need to generate ideas quickly. Use the spider-diagram* below and add as many ideas of your own as you can:

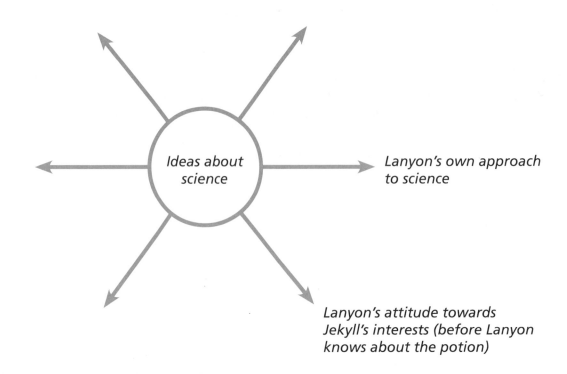

Ideas about science

Lanyon's own approach to science

Lanyon's attitude towards Jekyll's interests (before Lanyon knows about the potion)

*You can do this as a list if you wish.

PLANNING AN ESSAY

❸ Using **the ideas you generated**, write a simple **plan** with at least **five key points** (the first two have been done for you). Check back to your spider diagram or the list you made.

a) *Stevenson shows Lanyon rigorously following conventional scientific observation.*

b) *Lanyon and Jekyll are dismissive of each other's interests.*

c) ....

....

d) ....

....

e) ....

....

❹ Now list **five quotations**, one for each point (the first two have been provided for you):

a) *'the ebullition ceased and the compound changed to a dark purple' (p. 55)*

b) *Jekyll says Lanyon is 'a hide-bound pedant ... an ignorant blatant pedant. I was never more disappointed in any man' (p. 17)*

c) ....

....

d) ....

....

e) ....

....

❺ Now read this task and write a **plan** of your own, including **quotations**, and continue on a separate sheet of paper.

Read the passages from *'Mr Utterson the lawyer'* to *'they implied no aptness in the object'* (p. 1) and from *'And the lawyer set out homeward'* (p. 15) to *'the strange clauses of the will'* (p. 16).

Question: *How does Stevenson present Mr Utterson?*

....

....

....

....

....

....

....

PROGRESS LOG [tick the correct box]   Needs more work ☐   Getting there ☐   Under control ☐

Sample answers

OPENING PARAGRAPHS

Read this task:

Question: *How does Stevenson depict the relationship between Dr Jekyll and Mr Utterson?*

Now look at these two alternative openings to the essay and read the examiner comments underneath:

Student A

> *In this extract, Stevenson shows Mr Utterson being worried about Dr Jekyll's will and wanting to find out if Jekyll is OK or if he is being pressured. Utterson is a good friend to Jekyll, and stands by him through all his problems. Jekyll doesn't want him to interfere, but Utterson is too worried to leave him alone.*

Student B

> *We see what Utterson is like right at the beginning. He is 'dusty, dreary, yet somehow lovable'. This makes him a bit odd as a friend. We see him as a friend to his cousin Enfield, and see how he behaves with him. Then we see him with Lanyon and they talk about Jekyll. Later, we see Utterson and Jekyll together. Stevenson has lots of chances to show us what Utterson thinks of Jekyll.*

❶ Which comment belongs to which answer? Match the paragraph (A or B) to the expert's feedback (1 or 2).

Expert viewpoint 1: This opening begins by describing Utterson and then explains how we see him with other people. This could be relevant to the essay, but is not an appropriate opening and is not related to the question.

Expert viewpoint 2: This is a clear opening paragraph that outlines some important aspects of the relationship between Jekyll and Utterson. It should be written in a more formal style, and the information presented in a linked and logical way, outlining the direction the essay will take.

Student A: .... Student B: ....

❷ Now it's your turn. Write the opening paragraph to this task on a separate sheet of paper:

Question: *Examine the roles of two minor characters in the novella.*

Think about:

- What function the characters play in the plot
- How Stevenson uses characterisation to suit each character's function.

Remember:

- Introduce the topic in general terms, perhaps **explaining** or **'unpicking'** the **key words** or **ideas** in the task (such as 'examine').
- Mention the **different possibilities** or ideas that you are going to address.
- Use the **author's name**.

*AO4 is assessed by OCR only.

WRITING ABOUT TECHNIQUES

Here are two paragraphs in response to a different task, where the students have focused on the writer's techniques. The task is:

Read from: *'Nearly a year later'* (p. 20) to *'the maid fainted'* (p. 21).

Question: *How does Stevenson use voice and narrative perspective in this extract and in the novella as a whole?*

Student A

The maid doesn't have anything to say directly in this passage but the murder is told to us in the way she saw it. She was in her room and looking out of the window, so she was the only witness. We get an idea of what she says when she talks about the event because Stevenson says 'Never (she used to say...)' which summarises what the maid says.

Student B

Stevenson relates the murder from the point of view of the maid, who was the only witness to it. The narrator refers to the maid reporting the event later, and so we assume that the account is a summary of her words. The maid is described as 'romantically given', and this ties in with the tone of the account, which refers to Carew as 'an aged and beautiful gentleman' with 'a very pretty manner of politeness' – these are not phrases the narrator would use but paint an effective picture of the maid and her view of events.

Expert viewpoint 1: This high-level response explains how Stevenson uses voice to give an impression of the maid's words. It relates the statement about the maid's character, 'romantically given', to the way the account is presented, and shows how Stevenson sets the scene for summarising her view. The quotations are relevant and competently embedded.

Expert viewpoint 2: This mid-level response shows some grasp of how Stevenson is using language to convey the maid's point of view, but it does not zoom in on particular words or phrases which demonstrate this. It shows how Stevenson introduces the idea of the maid relating events. It could be written more fluently.

❸ Which comment belongs to which answer? Match the paragraph (A or B) to the expert's feedback (1 or 2).

Student A: .... **Student B:** ....

❹ Now, take another **aspect** of the scene and on a separate sheet of paper write your own **paragraph**. You could **comment** on one of these aspects:

● How the words chosen by Stevenson reflect the maid's character or frame of mind

● How the account seems to be phrased as an explanation to the police

● Whether the maid's voice is used consistently

Now read this **lower-level** response to the following task:

Read from: '*It is useless, and the time awfully fails me*' (p. 73) to '*I bring the life of that unhappy Henry Jekyll to an end*' (p. 74).

Question: *How does Stevenson present the identity of Jekyll/Hyde at the end of the novella?*

Student response

> *In these final paragraphs of Jekyll's last statement, Jekyll completely jumbles up the way he talks about himself. He says 'I', 'us both', 'Jekyll' and 'Hyde'. It looks like he doesn't know who he is any more.*
>
> *At the end, he says 'I bring the life of that unhappy Henry Jekyll to an end.' So here it's confusing who 'I' is supposed to be. As a dual character, Jekyll is two people – Jekyll and Hyde, but it looks like Stevenson has got mixed up here as there is another 'I'.*

Expert viewpoint: The quotation in paragraph two is well chosen but is not embedded in a sentence. The response recognises the confusion over identity in the passage but does not explore its implications or relate it to Jekyll's state of mind. The student needs to explore what effect Stevenson achieves and how. The language in the response is sometimes too informal, as in 'jumbles up', and the student suggests Stevenson has got 'mixed up' rather than investigating why Stevenson might have used this technique.

⑤ **Rewrite** these two **paragraphs** in your own words, improving them by addressing:

- The lack of development of linking of points – no **'zooming in'** on **key words and phrases**
- The lack of **quotations** and **embedding**
- Unnecessary **repetition**, poor **specialist terms** and use of **vocabulary**

Paragraph 1:

In this passage, Stevenson shows Jekyll ....

....

and also ....

....

This implies that ....

....

Paragraph 2:

In the final line of the passage ....

....

However ....

....

This suggests ....

....

....

....

⑥ Write a **full-length response** to this exam-style task on a separate sheet of paper. Answer both parts of the question:

Question: *How does Stevenson depict Jekyll's changing attitude towards Hyde over the course of the novella?*

Write about:

● How Jekyll's attitude towards Hyde changes

● How Stevenson presents Jekyll's attitude

Remember to do the following:

● Plan **quickly** (no more than five minutes) what you intend to write, jotting down **four or five supporting quotations**.

● Refer closely to the **key words** in the question.

● Make sure you comment on **what** the writer does, the **techniques** he uses and the **effect** of those techniques.

● Support your points with **well-chosen quotations** or other evidence.

● Develop your points by **'zooming in'** on particular **words** or **phrases** and explaining their **effect**.

● Be **persuasive** and **convincing** in what you say.

● Check carefully for **spelling**, **punctuation** and **grammar**.

PROGRESS LOG [tick the correct box]   Needs more work ☐   Getting there ☐   Under control ☐

Further questions

① How does Stevenson explore what it is to be human in the novella?

② To what extent could *Dr Jekyll and Mr Hyde* be described as Gothic?

③ Explore the role of three minor characters in the novella. How does Stevenson depict these characters?

④ Is it fair to say that *Dr Jekyll and Mr Hyde* is a novella 'about' duality?

⑤ What structural role does Utterson play in the novella?

PROGRESS LOG [tick the correct box]   Needs more work ☐   Getting there ☐   Under control ☐

ANSWERS

Note: Answers have been provided for most tasks. Exceptions are 'Practice tasks' and tasks which ask you to write a paragraph or use your own words or judgement.

PART TWO: PLOT AND ACTION [PP. 8–30]

Chapter One: Story of the Door [pp. 8–9]

1 a) F; b) T; c) F; d) F; e) F; f) T; g) T

2 a) They are distant relations who take regular walks together. They seem ill-matched, and often walk in silence, but both value their excursions.

b) The area is bright and cheery, with attractive shops that are well looked-after, but the door is plain, battered and damaged by tramps and children.

c) Everyone feels extreme, unaccountable hatred towards him and most want to kill him. Enfield says that he looks deformed and is repellent, but he can't say why.

3

Point/Detail	Evidence	Effect or explanation
1: The narrator gives a description of Utterson's physical appearance.	'lean, long, dusty, dreary and yet somehow lovable.'	Our immediate impression is that he is cold and dull – but the phrase 'yet somehow lovable' raises our interest in him.
2: Utterson keeps his own pleasures in check, but is tolerant and even envious of others who feel able to have a good time.	'though he enjoyed the theatre, he had not crossed the doors of one for twenty years.'	He is strict with himself but easy-going with other people and slow to pass judgement – these will be important in his dealings with the other characters later.
3: Utterson does not judge people, or drop them if they fall on hard times.	'it was frequently his fortune to be … the last good influence in the lives of down-going men'	He is tolerant and helpful; this prepares the ground for his later behaviour towards Dr Jekyll.

Chapter Two: Search for Mr Hyde [pp. 10–11]

1 a) it provides for Jekyll's disappearance as well as his death

b) if he knows who Hyde is

c) he is worried that Jekyll is being blackmailed

d) he thinks Utterson has lied to him

2 a) He does not like the turn Jekyll's scientific work has taken, which he considers to be too 'fanciful.' He calls Jekyll's interests 'unscientific balderdash' (p. 10).

b) He is relieved; he has been disconcerted by seeing Hyde and is feeling a sense of menace in the flickering firelight and shadows.

c) He suspects that Hyde has found out about something Jekyll did wrong in the past and is blackmailing him about it. He fears that Hyde might kill Jekyll to benefit from his will.

3

Point/Detail	Evidence	Effect or explanation
1: Hyde is not attractive, but his physical appearance does not account for the unease that Utterson feels.	'not all of these together could explain the … disgust, loathing and fear with which Mr Utterson regarded him.'	This creates a sense of mystery, suspense and unease for us as readers.
2: Utterson feels that Hyde is somehow deformed, but cannot say how.	'he gave an impression of deformity without any nameable malformation'	The lack of detail is unsettling and allows us to imagine Hyde in any way that we would find repellent.
3: When we hear Utterson's own voice on the topic of Hyde, it is uncharacteristically emotional.	'God bless me, the man seems hardly human!'	By using Utterson's own voice Stevenson emphasises the oddity of Hyde, as Utterson is usually mild and slow to judge people.

Chapter Three: Dr Jekyll was Quite at Ease [pp. 12–13]

1 Utterson stays behind after dinner because he wants to talk to Jekyll about his **will**. Jekyll begins talking about Lanyon. Although this looks like a distraction, it is important as it gives the other side of the **dispute/argument** between Jekyll and Lanyon. Jekyll considers Lanyon to be **ignorant** and pedantic. Jekyll is **defensive** when Utterson begins to talk about Hyde. He claims he can be **rid** of Hyde whenever he wants to, but begs Utterson to **help** Hyde when Jekyll has disappeared. Utterson is reluctant but agrees.

2 Write **one** or **two sentences** in response to each of these questions:

a) They enjoy Utterson's company. He is a quiet man, and they like to sit peacefully with him for a while – it makes an easy transition between a lively evening and the silent solitude when everyone has gone.

b) Jekyll looks horrified, his face going pale. He becomes defensive and does not want to talk about Hyde and the will.

c) He is agreeing to let the matter about Hyde rest as Jekyll has asked him to. He wants to mend any rift between them so that he and Jekyll do not fall out.

3

Point/Detail	Evidence	Effect or explanation
1: Jekyll is keen not to offend Utterson while refusing his help.	'this is very good of you, this is downright good of you'	Jekyll needs Utterson to be on his side as he is relying on him to carry out the terms of his will.
2: Jekyll is evasive, and Stevenson uses this to increase the mystery and suspense.	'my position is a very strange – a very strange one.'	As Jekyll tries to withhold information, we become more curious to know what it is.
3: Jekyll responds with 'a certain incoherency of manner' which Stevenson conveys in the way that Jekyll speaks.	'it isn't what you fancy; it is not so bad as that'	His speech is abrupt and faltering, broken up into short phrases, and repetitive. In this way, Stevenson shows Jekyll's anxiety and confusion.

Chapter Four: The Carew Murder Case [pp. 14–15]

1 a) Mr Hyde; b) Sir Danvers Carew; c) Inspector Newcomen; d) the maid; e) the landlady; f) Dr Jekyll; g) Utterson

2 a) She has gone up to bed and is sitting by the window looking out into the street. The scene is lit by moonlight and takes place under her window.

b) Carew was carrying a letter addressed to Utterson and they found this on his body.

ANSWERS

c) It is well furnished with good quality linen, carpets and silver. There is a painting on the wall and a stock of fine wine.

3

Point/detail	Evidence	Effect or explanation
1: Stevenson describes how the fog swirls and changes, and is not a constant thick blanket.	'Mr Utterson beheld a marvellous number of degrees and hues of twilight.'	The movement and patchiness of the fog make it possible for Utterson to catch fleeting glimpses of the scene it hides.
2: The fog makes daytime as dark as night.	'lamps … had been kindled afresh to combat this mournful reinvasion of darkness'	The place feels unnatural and sinister, as though the normal world order has been overturned.
3: Stevenson describes the fog in a way that makes things unclear and inconsistent.	'like a district of some city in a nightmare.'	It adds to the Gothic atmosphere of the tale, and reflects Utterson's struggle to see what is happening.

Chapter Five: Incident of the Letter [pp. 16–17]

1 a) T; b) T; c) F; d) F; e) F; f) T; g) F

2 a) Because the handwriting is very similar to Jekyll's, suggesting Jekyll deliberately tried to disguise his handwriting; there was no envelope; Poole said no letters had been delivered by hand.

b) He is curious, as he has not been there before. But he finds it rather distasteful and strange, as it is messy and gloomy.

c) He is shocked and ill, looking 'deadly pale' (p. 25), but says he is no longer concerned about Hyde – he is worried about how it might reflect on his own character.

3

Point/detail	Evidence	Effect or explanation
1: The laboratory was once a dissecting theatre, but is presented by Stevenson as livelier then than now.	'once crowded with eager students and now lying gaunt and silent'	The contrast between the room's gloominess now and the dissecting theatre is surprising and sets the scene for dismal events.
2: The room is not cosy; it is full of equipment, is dimly lit and has barred windows.	'looking out upon the court by three dusty windows barred with iron.'	The bars make us think of a prison and the phrasing Stevenson has used, 'barred with iron', has a harsh sound of finality. Jekyll sounds trapped.
3: The fire and lamps are lit, yet still the room is dark and cold.	'even in the houses the fog began to lie thickly'	The gloom cannot be dispelled even indoors – this reflects Jekyll's state of mind.

Chapter Six: Remarkable Incident of Dr Lanyon [pp. 18–19]

1 a) sociable and charitable; b) afraid he is going to die; c) is responding to Utterson's letter; d) he does not like the gloomy atmosphere

2 a) Utterson thinks Lanyon is terminally ill and, being a doctor, knows what lies ahead and is unable to cope with it.

b) That he will now lead a solitary life and will not see Utterson often or leave his house. He says he has brought his troubles on

himself, but does not want to talk about them.

c) He gives a simple, brief factual account, which carries no emotion.

3

Point/detail	Evidence	Effect or explanation
1: Stevenson directs us to feel sympathy for Jekyll and find mystery in the letter.	'very pathetically worded, and sometimes darkly mysterious'	Stevenson alerts us to what we should look out for in the letter.
2: Jekyll sets out his desire to be alone and says he will not give his reasons for it.	'You must suffer me to go my own dark way … respect my silence.'	By drawing attention to what will not be revealed Stevenson creates a sense of mystery.
3: Jekyll speaks extravagantly of the horror of his situation, but gives no details.	'I could not think that this earth contained a place for sufferings and terrors so unmanning'	Unspecified horrors are more frightening than anything that is spelled out.

Chapter Seven: Incident at the Window [pp. 20–1]

1 Utterson is walking with Enfield, his **cousin**, when they come to the same door as they saw in their walk in Chapter One. Now, Enfield has discovered that the door is a back **entrance** to Jekyll's property and is **embarrassed** that he did not know it sooner. Jekyll is sitting at the window, but looks pale and **unwell**. He refuses to come out for a walk with them because he is **afraid**. While he is prepared to talk at the window, a look of **terror** crosses his face and he withdraws quickly. Utterson and Enfield are **horrified**.

2 a) Jekyll is afraid to leave his house, though we do not yet know why. He is sitting by a window, which we have already learned has bars across it.

b) It is late afternoon as there is 'premature twilight' (p. 34), but the sky is still bright overhead. It is early in the year (the events of the previous chapter took place in January), so twilight will come early in London.

c) He has seen something in Jekyll's face that fills him with horror. The thought of Jekyll's terrible suffering scares him.

3

Point/detail	Evidence	Effect or explanation
1: At first, Utterson tries to cheer Jekyll up, being jolly and encouraging.	'"You stay too much indoors," said the lawyer.'	Utterson is treating Jekyll's low mood lightly, suggesting that fresh air will make him feel better.
2: Jekyll introduces a hint of mystery in his refusal to leave his room, saying he is afraid to.	'it is quite impossible; I dare not.'	Jekyll does not give an explanation, so we wonder why it is that he is afraid to leave the room.
3: Stevenson quickly switches from a light tone to terror, as shown in the change in Jekyll's face.	'the smile was struck out of his face and succeeded by a look of such abject terror and despair'	Stevenson shows us what Utterson and Enfield see – the change in Jekyll, with no explanation. It is shocking because it is so sudden and unexplained, and we share their reaction.

The Strange Case of Dr Jekyll and Mr Hyde **73**

ANSWERS

Chapter Eight: The Last Night [pp. 22–3]

1 a) Bradshaw; b) Poole; c) the maid; d) Messrs Maw; e) Utterson; f) Jekyll; g) Hyde

2 a) Because his body is freshly dead, there is a crushed phial (tube for chemicals) in his hand and a smell of 'kernels', which is characteristic of the poison cyanide.

b) He considers it unseemly, and thinks that it would anger Jekyll.

c) It appears cosy and welcoming, with a burning fire, things laid out for tea and the kettle singing – but its ordinariness is disturbed by the twitching body of Hyde on the floor.

3

Point/detail	Evidence	Effect or explanation
1: Poole presents the mystery of who is in the cabinet by pointing out all that is odd.	'if that was my master, why had he a mask upon his face?'	Stevenson increases the sense of mystery by presenting facts in the form of questions.
2: Utterson gives an explanation that seems to remove the mystery.	'it is plain and natural, hangs well together and delivers us from all exorbitant alarms.'	The suspense seems removed as Utterson's explanation appears plausible and natural.
3: Poole reveals the man's height last; it demolishes Utterson's explanation.	[Jekyll] 'is a tall fine build of a man, and this was more of a dwarf.'	Suspense and mystery are intensified by Stevenson presenting and then overturning a rational explanation.

Chapter Nine: Dr Lanyon's Narrative [pp. 24–5]

Quick test

1 a) F; b) T; c) F; d) T; e) T; f) F; g) T

2 a) They recently had dinner together and Jekyll could then have told him anything he wanted to say to him. Lanyon can't imagine what Jekyll could have to say that would require a formal letter.

b) The letter from Jekyll seems so strange that he suspects Jekyll might be mentally disturbed, and perhaps dangerous.

c) His clothes are far too large for him, so his trousers have to be rolled up, and his coat hangs off his shoulders.

3

Point/detail	Evidence	Effect or explanation
1: Stevenson makes Lanyon give a very precise description of the potion.	'began … to effervesce audibly, and to throw off small fumes of vapour.'	This suits Lanyon's character as a practical scientist – he tries to give a detailed account of what he observes.
2: Hyde suggests that scientific knowledge can bring power.	'new avenues to fame and power shall be laid open to you'	He tempts Lanyon with the positive possibilities of scientific knowledge, knowing that Lanyon is curious.
3: Hyde uses wording that sounds like an ominous threat.	'your sight shall be blasted by a prodigy to stagger the unbelief of Satan.'	By using the words 'blasted' and 'Satan', Stevenson suggests that scientific knowledge can bring harmful outcomes as well as benefits.

Chapter Ten: Henry Jekyll's Full Statement of the Case [pp. 26–9]

1 *Jekyll tried to protect himself from discovery by renting rooms for Hyde in* **Soho**, *employing a* **landlady** *who would keep quiet and not complain about his behaviour. Jekyll also told his own* **staff** *that Hyde would be coming and going, and made a point of* **visiting** *his own house as Hyde so that they knew him. Jekyll made out his* **will** *in favour of Hyde and gave it to* **Utterson** *so that Hyde could still use his money if Jekyll* **disappeared**.

2 a) wants to appear upright and proper; b) terrible pain and sickness; c) sees his hand; d) Hyde kills Carew; e) could not get the right white powder

3 a) He recognises Hyde a part of himself and so feels 'a leap of welcome' (p. 61). He sees Hyde as natural and human as well as seeing 'pure evil' in him.

b) Hyde is wanted for the murder of Carew, and the penalty for murder at the time was to be hanged. He is also afraid of Hyde taking over and losing his identity as Jekyll.

c) He has run out of potion and knows that next time he changes into Hyde he will never be able to turn back again.

d) As Hyde is wanted for murder, he can't go to his own home now as Hyde because he would be recognised and his staff would call the police.

e) Every time he falls asleep he changes involuntarily into Hyde.

f) Hyde hates Jekyll and resents that he has to spend time as Jekyll, that Jekyll despises him, and that Jekyll could kill him by killing himself.

4

Point/detail	Evidence	Effect or explanation
1: Jekyll experiences terror at the moment of transformation.	'horror of the spirit that cannot be exceeded at the hour of birth or death.'	The experience is the equivalent of both a birth (of Hyde) and a death (of Jekyll).
2: Jekyll is thrilled to feel his new, evil self.	'the thought … braced and delighted me like wine.'	His thrill at discovering himself more evil is shocking, marking a change from his character as Jekyll.
3: Stevenson stresses the novelty of the released Hyde.	'the first creature of that sort'	This separation of the parts of the human has never happened before – it is presented as an exciting discovery.

7

Point/detail	Evidence	Effect or explanation
1: Jekyll's account switches from the first person ('I') to third person, talking about both Jekyll and Hyde as others.	'The powers of Hyde seemed to have grown with the sickliness of Jekyll.'	In this way Stevenson shows that Jekyll has lost track of himself, no longer knowing which identity the pronoun 'I' relates to.
2: Jekyll's account of his feelings about Hyde is full of vivid, physical imagery.	'closer than a wife, closer than an eye; lay caged in his flesh'	The images move from showing that they are linked to inextricably entangled, demonstrating how Jekyll could never separate from Hyde.
3: Jekyll describes Hyde in terms of things not living ('inorganic') but made to live.	'the slime of the pit seemed to utter cries and voices'	This creates a sense of horror, as it completely disrupts the natural order – as Jekyll has done.

PART THREE: CHARACTERS [PP. 31–41]

Who's who? [p. 31]

Dr **Henry** Jekyll

Mr **Gabriel John** Utterson

Mr **Edward** Hyde

Dr **Hastie** Lanyon

Poole

Inspector **Newcomen**

Dr Henry Jekyll [p. 32]

1 a) NEE; b) T; c) F; d) T; e) F; f) T; g) NEE

2 a) From early in his career, Jekyll wanted to be seen as respectable and upright.

b) Dr Lanyon considers Jekyll to be too fanciful, and not a serious scientist.

c) Mr Utterson worries that Jekyll is being blackmailed by Mr Hyde.

d) Jekyll is horrified at the prospect of turning into Hyde unexpectedly or staying as Hyde forever.

e) Jekyll's attitude to upsetting Lanyon by allowing him to witness the transformation is unconcerned and surprisingly callous.

Mr Edward Hyde [p. 33]

1, 2 repellent (p. 13); fiendish (p. 73); unfeeling (p. 3); energetic (p. 21); violent (p. 21); pleasure-seeking (p. 67); cruel (p. 67); uncontrolled (p. 67); life-loving (p. 73); secretive (p. 4)

3 *Mr Hyde is a manifestation of the **worst** aspects of Dr Jekyll's character, appearing when Jekyll takes a **potion**. He is not a normal human character. Jekyll describes him as being pure **evil**. He thinks only of his own **pleasure**, carrying out acts of **violence** without **concern** for others. He becomes **stronger** the more Jekyll takes the potion and his behaviour grows **worse**. Everyone who sees him finds him instantly and strangely **repulsive**.*

Mr Gabriel John Utterson [p. 34]

1

Quality	Evidence	Quotation(s)
Level-headed	Copes well in a crisis; remains calm in difficult situations.	'"Pull yourself together, Bradshaw," said the lawyer.' (p. 42)
Well-liked	His friends value him; he meets Enfield for regular walks.	'Where Utterson was liked, he was liked well.' (p.17)
Non-judgemental	He continues to see people who fall on hard times.	'he never marked a shade of change in his demeanour'. (p.1)
Jumps to conclusions	Decides Jekyll is being blackmailed; assumes Jekyll forged the letter from Hyde.	'"What!" he thought. "Henry Jekyll forge for a murderer!"' (p. 29)

2 'A great curiosity came on the trustee, to <u>disregard the prohibition</u> [2] and dive at once to the bottom of these mysteries; but <u>honour</u> [1] and faith to his dead friend were stringent obligations; and the <u>packet slept</u> [3] in the inmost corner of his private safe.' (p.33)

[1] *professional* – his job as lawyer demands that he subdue his curiosity

[2] *self-controlled* – he resists the temptation to read the letter

[3] *loyal* – he will obey Lanyon's wishes even after Lanyon's death

Dr Hastie Lanyon [p. 35]

1

His manner and appearance before his shock	1. *Initially jovial and sociable*
	2. *Robust and lively*
His attitude towards science	1. *Concerned with the practical and objective*
	2. *Initially dismisses Jekyll's interests*
His social position	1. *Respectable and well-thought of*
	2. *A successful doctor*

3 *Dr Lanyon was originally good **friends** with Jekyll, but disagreed with his approach to **science**. He considered Jekyll's approach too **fanciful**, but never imagined what Jekyll had succeeded in doing. When he witnesses Jekyll's **transformation** into Hyde after mixing his **potion**, Lanyon's worldview is so **challenged** he finds life **impossible**. Re-evaluating his view of what is **possible** is too much for him, and the shock kills him.*

Mr Richard Enfield [p. 36]

1, 2 confident (p. 4); just (p. 4); sociable (p. 2); fashionable (p. 2); observant (p. 6); popular (p. 2); active (p. 4); friendly (p. 2); talkative (p. 3)

3 *Enfield is Utterson's **cousin**. The pair take regular **walks** together, which they mostly pass in **silence**. People are surprised at their friendship as they are quite unlike each other, Utterson being quiet and sober while Enfield is considered a 'man about **town**'. In his dealings with Hyde he shows himself to be **confident** and forceful. He is active in pursuing **justice** in the form of compensation for the young girl's family.*

Poole [p. 37]

1

Quality	Evidence	Quotation(s)
a) Loyal	He has served Jekyll a long time and turns to Utterson for help for him.	'do you think I do not know my master after twenty years?' (p. 41)
b) Resourceful	He fetches Utterson to help on the last night, and suggests using an axe and poker to break the door down.	'There is an axe in the theatre' (p.41)
c) Articulate	His speeches are long and eloquent, vividly expressing his anxiety and distress.	'if that was my master, why had he a mask upon his face? If it was my master, why did he cry out like a rat...?' (p. 40)
d) Compassionate	He feels for Jekyll but is also moved by the sound of Hyde weeping.	'I came away with that upon my heart, that I could have wept too.' (p.43)

2 'Well, when that masked thing like a monkey jumped from among the chemicals and whipped into the cabinet, <u>it went down my spine like ice</u>.[2] 'O, I know it's not evidence Mr Utterson; <u>I'm book-learned enough for that</u>;[1] but a man has his feelings, and I give you my <u>bible-word</u>[3] it was Mr Hyde!' (p.42)

[1] *partly educated* – he knows enough to recognise a feeling is not legal evidence

[2] *frightened* – he openly expresses his fear

[3] *Christian* – he would swear on the Bible

ANSWERS

Mr Guest [p. 38]

1 a) F; b) NEE; c) T; d) F; e) NEE; f) T; g) F

2 a) Guest works for Mr Utterson as his head clerk.

b) Guest has frequently visited Jekyll's house (on business).

c) Guest changes his view of Hyde's sanity after looking at the letter.

d) Guest addresses Utterson as 'sir' because Utterson is his employer.

e) Guest's role in the novella is to reveal the letter from Hyde was written by Jekyll.

Inspector Newcomen and Sir Danvers Carew [p. 39]

1

Quality	Evidence	Quotation(s)
a) Ambitious	He sees a chance to advance his career in the Carew case.	'his eye lighted up with professional ambition.' (p. 21)
b) Confident	He assumes they will soon catch Hyde.	'I have him in my hand.' (p. 24)
c) Uneducated	His speech is informal and not grammatically correct.	'He don't seem a very popular character' (p. 23)
d) Efficient	He collects all the evidence he can from Hyde's rooms.	'the inspector disinterred the butt end of a green cheque book' (p. 24)

2 Sir Danvers Carew is seen only by the maid and described in the novella after his **death**. The maid says he is old and **beautiful**. From the way he behaves, he seems to be very **polite**. He was a friend and **client** of Utterson, and Utterson has a **high** opinion of him. As we trust Utterson's judgement, we are likely to accept this as **true**. Carew worked as an **MP**, so we would expect him to be **respectable**.

The maid and Hyde's landlady [p. 40]

1 a) T; b) F; c) T; d) T; e) F; f) T; g) NEE

2

a) The landlady has a pale face and silver-coloured hair.

b) The narrator suggests she is evil and a hypocrite.

c) She seems pleased to learn that Hyde is in trouble.

d) Jekyll employed her because she would keep quiet and not be concerned by Jekyll's odd behaviour.

e) The landlady's manners are good.

PART FOUR: THEMES, CONTEXTS AND SETTINGS [PP. 42–50]

Themes [pp. 42–5]

1 Robert Louis Stevenson often draws attention to social position and **reputation**. Jekyll says he was concerned to appear **respectable** and was **ashamed** of his pleasures. Hyde is willing to pay money to the girl's family because he is keen to avoid a **scene**. Utterson is sharp with Jekyll's servants for standing around together on the last night as he considers it **irregular** and unseemly. Poole addresses Mr Utterson as 'sir' but Utterson calls him 'Poole' because he considers himself Poole's social **superior**.

2 a) friendship; b) natural and unnatural; c) social standing; d) law; e) science

3 a) The main focus of duality is on the two aspects of human nature. These are explored through Jekyll's separation of his 'evil' aspect into Hyde.

b) There are many examples of events having a dual aspect, of things seeming to be one way and actually being another, such as

Utterson believing that Jekyll is being blackmailed by Hyde.

c) Jekyll's own house has a dual character, with a respectable front entrance to the main house and secret, battered door into the laboratory at the back.

d) Even before he started to take his potion, Jekyll felt he lived a double life because he kept his pleasures secret in order to appear respectable and to progress in his career.

4 a) Dr Lanyon's comment raises the theme of friendship. He and Jekyll have been old friends, but they have fallen out over their differing views of science. Lanyon's words recall the long-established friendship through the familiarity of Utterson and Enfield.

Stevenson shows: there is little affection between them now, but the wording is gentle – it doesn't suggest they have had a serious disagreement.

b) Poole's response to seeing Hyde briefly relates to the theme of what is natural and unnatural. His physical response is instinctive, and comes from his automatic feeling that Hyde is unnatural. Hyde has this effect on everyone.

Stevenson's effect: this makes us shudder, recreating the effect Poole describes, so that we actually feel Hyde's unnaturalness.

5 a) Utterson is associated with the theme of law. Stevenson shows Utterson as a lawyer, careful to act honourably, keeping documents without looking at them and obeying Jekyll's wishes. He helps the police to look for Hyde, but he also looks for evidence to use against Hyde, hoping to counter any blackmail Hyde is trying against Jekyll.

b) There are many cases when Hyde is referred to in terms of evil, the devil or hell. Stevenson also uses allusions, such as that to Dr Fell (p. 14), to strengthen the association. Hyde even uses such language himself, saying Lanyon will see a sight to 'stagger the unbelief of Satan' (p. 55).

c) Jekyll and Lanyon both follow and represent contrasting aspects of science. Jekyll represents and practices 'transcendental' science, but Lanyon practises and represents purely practical science, dismissing anything involving dabbling in the unknown.

6 a) In describing in detail what happens to the potion Hyde mixes, Lanyon tries to give an accurate and precise account. This reflects the way he watches in a detached way, as though everything is a science experiment he must describe accurately.

b) Jekyll has become more philosophical in his interests, dealing with larger questions about the nature of the human spirit. He still tries to address these through scientific experiments.

c) Poole doesn't understand the science or want to know about it, he is just sent by Jekyll to different chemists to try to buy the right powder. His use of the word 'stuff' shows that he does not know how to describe it properly.

7

Point/detail	Evidence	Effect or explanation
1: Utterson feels instantly repelled by Hyde.	'the hitherto unknown disgust, loathing and fear with which Mr Utterson regarded him'	Disgust, loathing and fear are strong responses and have more impact because Utterson is a mild man.
3: Utterson finds something subhuman about Hyde.	'God bless me, the man seems hardly human!'	This suggests he is either animal or supernatural. Either way he appears unnatural.
3 Hyde is linked with the Devil by the language Stevenson uses.	'if ever I read Satan's signature upon a face'	The reference to a signature suggests ownership – Satan owns Hyde, he is not a self-determining character.

Contexts [pp. 46–7]

1 a) fog; b) London; c) Gothic fiction; d) the Victorian age; e) recent scientific developments; f) a lawyer

2 a) It proposes that humans are a type of animal and descended from apes, challenging ideas of what it is to be human. Hyde acts entirely on his 'animal' instincts, suggesting that Jekyll has split off the baser, more animal-like or natural part of himself.

b) Guest is an expert in graphology, a popular pseudo-science in the nineteenth century. It claims that a person's character is revealed in their handwriting.

c) Utterson is a lawyer and is charged with carrying out Jekyll's will, a legal document. He is also trusted as a witness and to read the formal statements of Lanyon and Jekyll.

3 Complete this table:

Point/detail	Evidence	Effect or explanation
1: *Stevenson uses vivid, flamboyant language.*	*'a grinding in the bones, deadly nausea, and a horror of the spirit'*	*Extreme and extravagant language is a common feature of Gothic literature, and is designed to inspire horror in the reader.*
2: *Events seem to be unnatural or supernatural.*	*'I was suddenly aware that I had lost in stature.'*	*Supernatural events and mystery are central to the Gothic tradition.*
3: *Stevenson creates a sense of shock by showing Jekyll delighting in recognising his evil.*	*'I knew myself … to be more wicked … and the thought … delighted me.'*	*Unnatural and grotesque behaviour and responses are common in Gothic literature.*

Settings [pp. 48–9]

1 Dr Jekyll's house – front

Utterson goes in this way when he visits Jekyll

Dr Jekyll's house – back

Where Enfield tells Utterson about Hyde trampling the girl

Mr Utterson's house

Where Utterson keeps Jekyll's will and Lanyon's letter in his safe

Dr Lanyon's house

Where Hyde goes to collect the potion, where Utterson visits and where Lanyon witnesses the transformation

Mr Hyde's lodgings

Where Inspector Newcomen finds sufficient evidence to know that Hyde killed Sir Danvers Carew

2 a) It is set in London, which even in Victorian times was a large, sprawling city with very different areas, from smart to seedy. A large city makes it easy for Hyde to disappear. Stevenson creates a sense of menace by describing the deprived areas Utterson travels through to reach Hyde's house.

b) The fog makes the setting eerie and threatening. It makes it difficult for people to see clearly what it is going on; they just get flashes through the fog. This reflects the way the whole novel is written, as we see very little until near the end.

c) It has a respectable front door and a run-down back door. The front door is associated with Jekyll and the back door with his *alter ego*, Hyde. The main part of the house is comfortable and looked after by servants, but the laboratory is untidy and cluttered; it used to be a dissecting theatre, so has a gloomy past.

3 a) To get from Jekyll's house to his cabinet, it is necessary to cross a yard that was once a garden, walk through the laboratory and up some stairs, then go through a red baize door.

b) On the last night, Jekyll's cabinet has contrasting elements. It has a cosy feel, with a lit fire, a singing kettle and tea things set out, but some precious objects have been vandalised and the dead body of Hyde lies on the floor.

c) Hyde's rooms also have a dual aspect, which Stevenson presents by showing that there is good quality furniture and pictures, but the place is in disarray and has been ransacked.

PART FIVE: FORM, STRUCTURE AND LANGUAGE [PP. 51–7]

Form [p. 51]

1 a) The novella is related by several narrators.

b) A novella is a story that is shorter than a novel.

c) *Dr Jekyll and Mr Hyde* is told in the order Utterson learns about events.

d) Letters, written statements and other characters' reports presented in a story are called interpolated narratives.

e) In *Dr Jekyll and Mr Hyde*, we see some events before understanding them.

2 a) Stevenson uses extravagant and flamboyant language to create a sense of horror. The novella deals with strange, supernatural experiences and makes use of letters and other additional narratives to create different perspectives.

b) It is like a detective story in having a mystery to solve and involving a crime. It is unlike a detective story in that the mystery is not who committed the crime, and the mystery is not solved by following clues – clues lead nowhere in the novella, and the explanation comes from Jekyll.

c) He is able to tell events out of sequence to increase suspense and mystery. He is also able to give the personal responses and thoughts of different people, which he could not do with a single first-person narrator.

Structure [pp. 52–3]

1

Scene	Chapter
a: *Sir Danvers Carew is murdered.*	*Four*
b: *Poole and Utterson break down a door.*	*Eight*
c: *Utterson and Enfield take their second walk.*	*Seven*
d: *Hyde tramples a small girl.*	*One*
e: *Lanyon witnesses the action of the potion on Hyde.*	*Nine*
f: *Utterson visits Lanyon and finds him unwell.*	*Six*

2 a) He is able to build suspense and mystery by presenting unexplained events that arouse our curiosity.

b) He uses them to present information that could not be given by any of the main characters, such as events that happened while no main characters (except Hyde) were present.

c) Stevenson shows us situations becoming more serious or changing. For example, Hyde's second attack is more violent than the first and it builds the sense of menace.

3

Point/Detail	Evidence	Effect or explanation
1: *Stevenson introduces the idea that something shocking will happen.*	*'what follows is under the vows of your profession … behold!'*	*The word 'behold' is a command to watch, and is associated with wonderful sights.*

ANSWERS

2: *The progress of the change is presented in detail, but without explanation.*	*'he seemed to swell – his face became suddenly black'*	*We can picture what is happening and want to know its outcome and meaning.*
3: *The important revelation comes right at the end of the paragraph.*	*'there stood Henry Jekyll!'*	*This comes as shock, since we imagine changes, but not a change into Jekyll.*

Language [pp. 54–5]

1

Word/expression	Meaning
a) penny number	fire [d]
b) juggernaut	drop [g]
c) bland	pamphlet [a]
d) conflagration	filmy [f]
e) countenance	unremarkable [c]
f) diaphonous	face [e]
g) minim	chariot [b]

3

Feeling	Moment in the novella	Quotation
1: Horror	1: *When Lanyon sees Hyde turn into Jekyll*	*'"O God!" I screamed, and "O God!" again' (p. 56)*
2: Curiosity	2: *When Utterson wants to see Hyde*	*'If he could but once set eyes on him, he thought the mystery would lighten' (p. 11)*
3: Anxiety	3: *When Poole is afraid that Jekyll has been murdered*	*'"I don't like it, sir – I wish I may die if I like it."' (p. 36)*

4 a) disbelieving; b) irritated; c) brisk; d) hopeful

5 Utterson initially takes a superior tone with Poole, reflecting his view of their different social positions and the unlikely tale Poole tells him, but as he sees that it is true he speaks to him more as an ally and an equal.

6

Example of quotation	Literary technique	Meaning/effect
'the animal within me licking the chops of memory' (p. 69)	*Imagery*	*Stevenson makes the image of Hyde as an animal much more vivid by causing us to think of an animal licking around its mouth after eating.*
'If that was my master, why had he a mask upon his face?' (p. 40)	*Rhetorical question*	*Poole asks a question to which he does not expect an answer; he does this to imply that it can't be Jekyll because Jekyll wouldn't wear a mask.*
'these powers should be dethroned from their supremacy' (p. 59)	*Personification*	*Jekyll speaks of the powers that make up his spirit as though they were a king that sat on a throne.*

7

Technique	Example	Effect
1: *Long, convoluted sentences*	*'You should be back, if you set out at once …'*	*This follows Jekyll's train of thought, which is tortured, confused and anxious.*
2: *Metaphor*	*'the shipwreck of my reason'*	*The image of disaster and devastation is a quick, vivid way of showing how terrible Jekyll's fate will be.*
3: *Personal address*	*'Serve me, my dear Lanyon'*	*The personal appeal carries extra weight because Jekyll uses Lanyon's name and the affectionate term 'my dear' it makes it harder for him to refuse.*

PART SIX: PROGRESS BOOSTER [PP. 58–67]

Expressing and explaining ideas [pp. 58–9]

2 Student A: Level – High

Why? *The student has used properly embedded quotations to support a good point about Utterson's character and how it is shown.*

Student B: Level – Mid

Why? *The student has made a good point about Utterson but has written too informally about it and has not presented the quotation well or talked about its effects.*

3 *The phrase 'forge for a murderer' suggests that Utterson feels very strongly – it is very powerful and dramatic, bringing two serious crimes together in simple, effective language. It's very different from the formal, quite complicated sentence patterns usually associated with Utterson.*

4, 5, 6 *Lanyon* **asserts** *that Jekyll is 'one whom I consider dead' which* **demonstrates** *that he wants nothing more to do with him. He then* **states** *that 'Nothing can be done' to repair their friendship, which effectively* **signals** *to Utterson that he must stop trying to help. Lanyon* **tells** *Utterson that he can stay if he is willing to talk about something else. This* **makes clear** *that he still likes Utterson.*

Making inferences and interpretations [p. 60]

1 *When Hyde comes to Dr Lanyon's consulting room to find the drawer of chemicals, he is at first too eager and impatiently puts his hand on Lanyon's arm.* Lanyon is irritated, but with an effort remains polite. When he says to Hyde 'You forget that I have not yet had the pleasure of your acquaintance' he uses a stock polite phrase without meaning it. He does not really think there will be any pleasure in knowing Hyde, and indeed in the same sentence mentions his 'horror' at Hyde's presence.

2 c) *… he is unwilling to accept responsibility for the acts he committed as Hyde.*

Writing about context [p. 61]

1 a) *Because it shows how Stevenson uses social position to guide our expectations in this part of the plot.*

2 c) *Dr Lanyon says that his life is 'shaken to its roots' by what he has seen, which is how many people felt about the way science had assaulted their long-held beliefs about the world.*

Structure and linking of paragraphs [pp. 62–3]

1 _Stevenson never shows Hyde relating to other people in any way other than self-interest._ Jekyll says that 'Hyde was indifferent to Jekyll' (p. 66). In saying this, Jekyll means that Hyde neither likes nor dislikes Jekyll, though he later becomes afraid that Jekyll might kill himself and so put an end to Hyde, which is another selfish motive.

3 _Jekyll says that he was already committed to 'a profound duplicity in life', but once he begins to take his potion he goes from duplicity to duality, living as two different people. At first, he sees Hyde as part of himself that has been freed to act independently. But soon the border between his identity and Hyde's becomes blurred. He can no longer control which form he takes and his real identity becomes lost._ Stevenson shows this through having Jekyll refer to both Jekyll and Hyde in the third person in his statement, implying that Jekyll no longer identifies as himself, or 'I'.

Writing skills [pp. 64–5]

3 Jekyll finds **accommodation** for Hyde in a **dismal** area of Soho **where** no one will take much notice of him. His **landlady** is **unscrupulous** and Jekyll trusts her not to **interfere** in what **Hyde** does there.

4 Stevenson presents the law through two characters, Mr Utterson and Inspector Newcomen. **Being** a lawyer is **Utterson's** job, so he is supposed to know and uphold the law. This makes it surprising when he hints that he might look into **Hyde's** past to see if he can find anything to blackmail him about, saying he 'must have secrets of his own; black secrets by the look of him'.

5 Student B

6 Stevenson **uses** very flamboyant language with lots of imagery in Jekyll's final statement. Jekyll **is trying** to get across very difficult, unfamiliar ideas that he **knows** people **will struggle** with. To make them clearer, he **uses** imagery that **evokes** pictures of things that **are** more familiar.

Tackling exam questions [p. 66]

1 Question: <u>How</u> does <u>Stevenson present contrasting ideas about science</u> in the novella?

Write about:

- <u>Different ideas about science</u> that are shown
- How <u>Stevenson shows</u> them

Planning an essay [p. 67]

3, 4

c) Jekyll's research is into more mystical areas.

'the direction of my scientific studies, which led wholly towards the mystic and the transcendental' (pp. 57–58)

d) The challenge to his view of science is more than Lanyon can bear.

'"I have had a shock," he said, "and I shall never recover."' (p. 31)

e) Stevenson suggests some scientific knowledge is too dangerous to know.

'"I sometimes think if we knew all, we should be more glad to get away."' (p. 31)

Sample answers [pp. 68–71]

1 Student A: Expert viewpoint 2; Student B: Expert viewpoint 1

3 Student A: Expert viewpoint 2; Student B: Expert viewpoint 1